Ella at the Well

Lorna Hill wrote her first stories in an exercise book after watching Pavlova dance in Newcastle. Her daughter, Vicki, aged ten, discovered one of these stories and was so delighted by it that Lorna Hill wrote several more and soon they were published. Vicki trained as a ballet dancer at Sadler's Wells and from her letters Mrs Hill was able to glean the knowledge which forms the background for the 'Wells' stories.

Ella at the Wells tells the story of Ella Sordy, an orphan from a little mining village in Northumberland, whose whole life is changed when her talent is spotted by the great ballerina, Veronica Weston . . .

Sadler's Wells

Lorna Hill

Ella
at the Wells

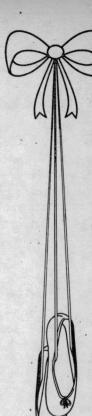

Piper Books

To
CYRIL BEAUMONT
in gratitude for the help
his books on ballet have
been to me

First published 1954 by Evans Brothers Ltd
This Piper edition published 1989 by Pan Books Ltd,
Cavaye Place, London SW10 9PG
9 8 7 6 5 4 3
© Lorna Hill 1954
ISBN 0 330 28617 X
Phototypeset by Input Typesetting Ltd, London
Reproduced, printed and bound in Great Britain by
Richard Clay Ltd, Bungay, Suffolk

Contents

SCOTT FAMILY TREE

SIR ADAM SCOTT = **MAUREEN O'ROURKE**
(Sebastian's Irish Grandmother)

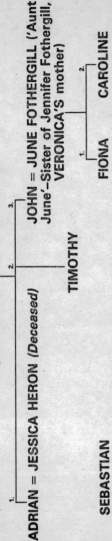

1. **ADRIAN** = **JESSICA HERON** *(Deceased)*

2. **TIMOTHY**

3. **JOHN** = **JUNE FOTHERGILL** ('Aunt June'–Sister of Jennifer Fothergill, VERONICA'S mother)

SEBASTIAN

1. **FIONA**

2. **CAROLINE**

MONKHOUSE FAMILY TREE

SIR NIGEL MONKHOUSE = **ISABELLA RENWICK**
(of Bychester Tower)

1. **ROBERT** = **JUDITH RISDALE**

NIGEL

2. **CAROL** ('Aunt Carol') = **HAROLD FOSTER**
[He is the brother of IRMA FOSTER, ballerina, who married Oscar Devereux. MARIELLA is their daughter]

JANE
(ballet dancer)

Part One

Chapter 1

Cinderella

One September night two monsters of steel and fire passed each other somewhere in the Midlands – the Caledonian flying north, and the Queen of Scots travelling south. Aboard the former, fast asleep in a first-class sleeping berth, lay Jane Foster, former ballerina of the Sadler's Wells Ballet Company. On the Queen of Scots, huddled in a corner of a third-class compartment, sat a pale, thin little girl. Her name was Ella Sordy, and two tears rolled slowly down the side of her nose, for she was very homesick. She was thirteen years old – nearly fourteen in fact – though you wouldn't have thought her more than ten or eleven, and this was the very first time she had been more than thirty miles away from her home in the north of England.

Yes, as one ballerina gave up her career as a dancer to take up another equally exacting one – that of marriage – another small girl set out, like Dick Whittington, to find fame and fortune in London. Little Ella Sordy was on her way to join the Sadler's Wells School, just as Jane Foster had left the Wells for ever!

For the moment let us leave Jane sleeping in her berth, and go back nine months or so to the day when Miss Ruth

Fisher, second-in-command of the Blackheath Council School, decided to stage a pantomime. Miss Fisher had wanted to read for a degree in English Literature, but she hadn't been quite clever enough to win a place at university, so she had done the next best thing: put in two years at a training college, and emerged with a Teaching Diploma. After this she had taught small children in various schools in the country, and now here she was teaching Standard Five – Ella Sordy, together with fifty-odd other children – in the Blackheath School.

Blackheath was a village. Not a collection of picturesque cottages, each with its little garden, bright with hollyhocks and pansies, church with tall spire, tree-shaded vicarage with rooks cawing, and all around the green countryside, which is what the word 'village' calls to mind. Blackheath wasn't a bit like that. To be sure, it lay in a fold of the moorland, near the borders of Durham and Northumberland, and there was country all around it, but here the resemblance ceased. There were ten thousand people in Blackheath, nearly all coal-miners and iron-foundry workers, and they lived in long rows of old pit cottages, huddled together at the foot of a crop of ominous black slag-heaps. On the hillside opposite, about half a mile away, a new village of clean, square, council houses had been built, but there was a long waiting list for them. Miss Fisher had lodgings there, but so far Ella Sordy's family hadn't been lucky. They still lived at number 113 Pit Street, which was near the end of one of the longest and most disreputable rows of the old cottages. Ruth Fisher often wondered how Ella managed to recognize her home when she got there, because all the houses were as alike as peas, from the clean white curtains at the small square windows (and how they were kept in that snowy condition was nothing short of a miracle, for the dust of the pit lay upon everything!) to the plant on a bamboo table, and the cardboard squirrel to keep down the flies, hanging above. When you got inside, the Sordys' cottage was much the same as everybody else's. An open fireplace, with a gleaming steel fender and 'tidy', and a huge blackleaded oven, took up one side of the living-room. Several pictures of the Royal Family occupied the wall opposite. An old wooden settle, heaped with patch-work and quilted cushions, stood under the window, and from the fourth wall a large photograph of the late Mr Alfred Sordy – the present Mr Sordy's father – glowered down from behind a large walrus moustache upon his descendants. In front of the glowing coal fire lay a 'hookie' mat with a large off-white cat upon it. How the cat, whose name was Snowball, managed to keep itself even off-white, considering that its playground consisted of pit-heaps, was another miracle!

To a stranger, Blackheath presented a somewhat awe-some spectacle with its black pit-heaps towering above the village like a range of satanic mountains. If it hadn't been for the great wheels and cranes, engine-houses, chimneys, and overhead railways with their tubs of coal swinging along, you might easily have thought you were looking up at the Cuillin Hills of Skye!

As we have already said, the New Estate was a long way from the actual colliery and the iron works, so that Ruth Fisher could only hear from afar the hiss of steam and the clank of machinery. The noise wasn't enough to distract her thoughts from this exciting idea of staging a pantomime for the after-Christmas festivities. Last year she had put on a musical version of *Aladdin*. She had called it an 'operetta', and it was composed entirely of rhymed-couplets, all made up by herself. When she had read it over (in a discreet undertone so that next door wouldn't hear, the walls of the council houses not being voice-proof!) it had sounded beauti-tiful. Yes, really beautiful, thought Ruth Fisher proudly. But alas, when she got together the brightest members of Standard Five and began to teach them the lines, they sounded anything but lovely. The Blackheath children *would* accent all the syllables alike, making the 'ands' and the 'thes' just as important as words like 'Aladdin' and 'jewels'.

> 'Aladdin looked *around* him and *descried*
> A *cave* with *jewels* massed on every side,'

said Miss Fisher.

'A-lad-in-looked-a-round-him-and-des-cried,' repeated the class in a monotonous chant, 'a-cave-with-jew-els-massed-on-ev-ry-side.'

'No! No! *No!*' cried Miss Fisher in despair. 'You mustn't *sing* it like that!'

But it was no use. From babyhood Blackheath had been taught to chant 'po-try', and it couldn't or wouldn't change now.

'Do you always say all the words "tum-te, tum-te, tum-te, *tum*" like that?' cried the exasperated mistress.

'Yes, miss!' shouted the class in one voice.

'And you never say any of them louder or softer than any of the rest?'

'No, miss!' shouted the class cheerfully.

'Oh, well – then I expect it can't be helped,' sighed Ruth. 'But next year it shall be a pantomime in the real sense of the word – mime, and no word spoken.' After all, she thought to herself, they can't go far wrong if they haven't a single word to speak! All I've got to do is to choose a few graceful children. . .

The year had gone past, and she had got the pantomime well under way. It was *Cinderella* and it was all either mimed or danced. The music was on tape, and Ruth had even written to her friend, Mary Martin, who owned the biggest ballet school in Newcastle, and persuaded her to send out a ballet student (at her, Ruth's, own expense) to coach the children in the dances. All that remained now was to choose the cast, and, most important, to decide who was to be Cinderella.

'The little girl who sits in the second row, over by the middle window. What's her name? . . . Yes, Ella Sordy. She's a graceful child – I've watched her in the school-yard at playtime, and she runs beautifully. I wonder if she could be Cinderella?' Ruth said to her friend and colleague, Jean Rutherford, who taught the infants and who shared her lodging.

'You mean that plain kid with the thin legs and the pale face?' said Jean. 'The one with a couple of sisters lower down in the school – Standard Three, or thereabouts . . . Well, of course, it's *your* show, darling, but don't you think that a rather *prettier* child would be better. What about Rosie Proud? She's quite a good little dancer. Can do "tap" like anything. She's good at singing, too. I heard her in *Jack and Jill* that the Women's Guild put on before Christmas. She was really good when she sang "Out in the rain with my cutie".'

Ruth Fisher shook her head. She knew exactly what she wanted and it wasn't the self-assured Rosie Proud singing her precocious songs, imitating a grown-up to the manner born, and doing 'tap'. Nor was it Annie Carr with her fat white legs and pink hair-ribbons, nor Susie Duffie with her china-blue eyes and cheeky manner, nor Mabel Butterfield with her handsome, coarse features (though possibly Mabel might do for Cinderella's stepmother, amended Ruth to herself). She didn't even want Elizabeth Ann Green, who talked in a mincing voice and was described as distinctly "better class" by Jean.

'No, I still think I'll try Ella Sordy,' she said at length.

'OK. It's your funeral!' laughed Jean. 'Well, I must be off. How you can be bothered with these theatricals I can't think! I should have thought you'd have had enough of kids by the time school was over. *I* certainly have! A game or two of badminton for me! Bye-bye!'

'Good-bye,' said Ruth absent-mindedly. Her mind was already back in her pantomime . . . Ella Sordy as Cinderella; Mabel Butterfield, the Stepmother; the Ugly Sisters . . . the Prince. . .

'Ella,' said Ruth Fisher next day after morning school. 'Do you think you could be Cinderella in my pantomime?'

Now here was a curious thing, thought Ruth afterwards. All the other fifty-odd kids would have said: 'Yes, miss,' pat as pat, as they always did when asked if they could do anything. Never hesitate, always say 'Yes, miss,' and think afterwards, was the motto of the Blackheath children. They 'Yes, miss-ed,' everybody – from their teachers (male and female) to the vicar's wife and the vicar himself. Even the bishop, when he came every three years for the Confirmation, was addressed as 'miss'. The strange thing was that Ella Sordy didn't act according to rule. She looked up at Miss Fisher with a pair of large, dark eyes, and said: 'Cinderella – you mean the fairy-story, miss? You mean *me* to be her – Cinderella, you mean?'

'Yes, you,' said Ruth.

'Oo – miss!' said little Ella Sordy.

'We start rehearsals after school tomorrow,' said Miss Fisher. 'There's a young lady coming from the ballet school to teach you how to dance.'

'You mean Cinderella's goin' to dance?' said Ella. 'Like in the *Pi'tcher Post?*'

'Yes, dance and mime, and *nothing* else,' said Ruth firmly.

Ella said nothing.

'You'll wear your gym shoes,' said Miss Fisher.

'Yes, miss,' said Ella. 'What time, miss?'

'Six o'clock,' said Ruth. 'And mind you aren't late.'

'No, miss – I'll not be,' said Ella.

12

Chapter 2

Pit Street

There were quite a lot of members of the Sordy family besides Ella. First of all, there was 'Me Mam' who was square, raw-boned, and angular, with hair of an uncompromising straightness, except when she went to the Parish Social each December, and Mrs Duffy-round-the-corner, who had been in a real hairdresser's shop before her marriage, gave it a perm which lasted a full three months, and altered Me Mam's appearance quite a lot.

Then there was 'Me Dad', who was a miner doing disability work since his accident in the pit many years ago. Then came the children – Our Lily, Our D'reen, and Our Sid. Our Sid had been the mainstay of the Sordy family after Me Dad's accident. Then he had met Gloria Stobbins at a 'hop' in the Co-operative Hall, and fallen in love with her. So they had got married, and Sid and Gloria had gone to live in Gloria's father's pub (which was the Dun Cow in the New Estate) so that Gloria could help her father in the bar at nights. Yes, there was no doubt about it, people said, when they beheld Gloria Sordy in her beaver-lamb coat, Sid Sordy had 'bettered' himself!

Now as to Ella, she wasn't a bit like the rest of the Sordy family, who were all the very spit and image of their mother – square, rosy-cheeked, raw-boned. Ella was tiny, with legs like sparrows' legs, and arms thin as matchsticks. Her hands and feet were tiny, and so was her pale face. The only big things about Ella were her enormous, velvety, dark eyes. You might have thought she was a changeling – a child left in the cradle by fairies in place of the Sordys' own square baby, and if you thought this, you wouldn't be far wrong, because, you see, Me Mam wasn't Ella's real mam. Who her real mam was, nobody knew for certain. Ella was one of the babies from the Cottage Homes, and Mrs Sordy had taken her to bring up when she was a few weeks old. Mrs Sordy remembered exactly when it was, because it was the year the big circus had come to Blackheath – the year Sid got engaged to Gloria. They'd all gone to the circus for a celebration, and right in the middle of the performance, a rumour had gone round that the trapeze artist's wife, who was having a baby, had tripped over some rope behind the Big Top, and had been taken to hospital. Next day it was all round the village that the woman had died in hospital during the night.

'Poor soul!' said Mrs Duffy, pausing in the act of pouring the neutralizer over a customer's hair. 'What a thing to happen! It just goes to show!'

'What about the bairn?' said Mrs Sordy who had come in to assist with the perm. 'What'll the bairn dee wi'oot its mam?'

'Oh, they'll tak it to the Cottage Homes,' said Mrs Duffy, 'for it stands to reason its dad canna dee wi' it. In a week or two mebbe someone'll adopt it.'

'*Never!* Neebody'd be such a fool as to adopt somebody else's bairn,' said Mrs Sordy. 'Noo keep still, Janet love! Ye dinna want to get the neutralizer doon your neck. It taks the colour oot o'your jumper somethin' awful!'

'They gets paid, a'course,' explained the knowledgeable Mrs Duffy. 'Quite a canny bit, and after all, it only drinks milk for the first month or two, and all the other things ye can get cheap at the clinic, and when it gans to school it gets a free dinner, and there's always the parish jumble for its clothes, so they'll be quite a tidy bit into pocket, I shouldn't wonder.'

14

Mrs Sordy suddenly became very thoughtful. It would be a blow to the household financially when Sid married his Gloria and took his wages up to the Dun Cow, and Dad on Disability and likely to be for the rest of his life. She didn't know how they would manage. When you've been used to a lot of money coming into the house, you miss it when it suddenly stops, a great deal more than if you've never had it in the first place.

'Dad,' said Mrs Sordy that night. 'What d'ye say if we tek a babby from the Cottage Homes?'

So that was how Ella came to be a member of the Sordy family. Nobody knew who she was, because the Authorities weren't allowed to tell, but common gossip said she was 'the Circus Babby'. At first, it is true, Mrs Sordy had taken Ella for the sake of the extra money she brought with her, but after a bit (even when two more babies of her own came along) she grew quite fond of her. In time she forgot completely that Ella wasn't her own child. She became 'Our Ella'. I won't pretend that Mrs Sordy was *quite* as fond of Ella as she was of Lily and D'reen, but that wasn't because Ella wasn't her own child, but because she was 'different'. She didn't always understand Ella. Sometimes she'd go mooning around, and you could get no sense out of her! You could give Lily or D'reen a slice of bread and jam and sixpence for the pi'tchers, and they'd be perfectly happy. But Ella – she'd rather sit and read a book any day. Not a comic, either, mind you, but real books that she got out of the school library, written by someone called Charles Dickens, with funny pictures.

'A lot of rubbish,' said Mrs Sordy to Mrs Rickerby, who lived next door. 'You should see them pi'tchers! Not like anything you ever saw! Men with great big heads on'em, and little wee legs like spiders! But they keep our Ella quiet. She's no bother is our Ella. Now our D'reen. . . Well, here they come! Talk o'the devil! They'll be wantin' their tea. Bye-bye, dearie!' The two neighbours said good-bye ceremoniously over their backyard walls and Mrs Sordy went indoors to welcome her family back from school.

They hurled themselves upon her, all talking at once, their voices shrill with excitement. Lily's voice, being the shrillest, came out on top.

'Mam! Mam! What d'you think's happened? Miss Fisher's chose our Ella for Cinderella in the pantomime! And D'reen and me's to be the Ugly Sisters!'

'Well, I never,' said Mrs Sordy. 'Our Ella! Who'd a thought it!'

'Yes, and Rosie Proud's mam is taking on terrible. Says Rosie oughta be Cinderella, and she won't let Rosie be in it at all, she says!'

'Well, I like her cheek!' observed Mrs Sordy. 'If you ask me, that Rosie's too smart by far, and her mam as well. Mebbe Miss Fisher's done well not to choose *her* for Cinder-ella, though why she couldn't have chose you or D'reen I don't know. You're both a whole lot prettier than our Ella.'

Meanwhile Ella stood lost in a dream. As Miss Fisher had explained the idea of the pantomime, she saw it in her imagination – Cinderella in her drab kitchen, wishing, wishing for a lovely dress to wear for the ball. One with spangles on it, thought Ella, like the spangles on the cobwebs when they went out to look for brambles.

'What are you standing there for, Ella?' demanded Mrs Sordy. 'You look proper moon-struck! Don't you want no tea?'

Ella looked down at the inch-thick slice of bread and jam lying on the oilcloth in front of her, and shook her head.

'I'm not hungry,' she said. 'Our Lily can have it.'

Our Lily did have it, and several more slices besides. There was nothing choosy or temperamental about Our Lily. Though she *had* been chosen for one of the Ugly Sisters instead of Cinderella, she wasn't losing her appetite over it!

'Is there a lot of recitin' po-try?' demanded Mrs Sordy, remembering last year's show, and the job she had had making D'reen and Lily learn their words.

'There's nawt to say,' said Lily. 'It's all music and dancin', and summat called "mime".'

'Like this,' put in Ella, running over to the portrait of Grandfather Sordy and holding out her thin little hands. 'I'm Cinderella, you see, and I'm cold, so I'm trying to warm my hands in front of the fire.'

'Dinna be daft!' said Mrs Sordy. 'There ain't no fire there. That's Grandad's photy!'

'Of *course* there isn't no fire,' explained Ella. 'It's all pretend, don't you see?'

'Bats, if you ask me!' said Mrs Sordy. 'I always said that Miss Fisher had a tile off! How can you have a panto without songs? Dancin's all very well, but—'

'What's that about dancin'?' said a voice from the door.

'Oh, come in, Mrs Dickson.' Mrs Sordy's neighbour on the other side stood there, arms akimbo. 'We was just talking about the teacher up at the school. Fair struck on dancin' she is. Wants our Ella for her pantomime, only there's nawt to say, only a lot of dances. Did ye ever hear the like?'

'Mebbe it's a new idea,' said Harriet Dickson. 'Like the bally. Take a peep at this.' She thrust a picture-paper dramatically in front of the teapot that Mrs Sordy had just set down on the table. 'D'ye see who 'tis?'

All the Sordys bent eagerly over the paper.

'Well, I don't see nothin' about dancin'—'

'There's that and more. Look at this.' Mrs Dickson pointed with her finger to a paragraph.

' "Northcountry Jottings," ' she read out aloud. ' "Young friends of Lady Blantosh of Blantosh Castle, Northumberland, go to Scottish Ball to support effort in

17

aid of destitute babies—" '

'Them's like our Ella,' put in Mrs Sordy. 'But what's it to do wi' us?'

'Dinna interrupt,' said Mrs Dickson. 'I was just gettin' to that. Where was I? – Oh, yes, "Destitute babies. Miss Mariella Foster, of Monks Hollow, Northumberland, and Mr Nigel Monkhouse of Bychester Tower talking to members of the Sadler's Wells Ballet – Miss Vivien Chaytor, and Mr Josef Linsk – at the Inveross Hotel where a ball was held to usher in Hogmanay. Miss Jane Foster, Sadler's Wells ballerina, should have been in the photograph, but she met with an unfortunate accident when climbing Ben Cruachan, one of Scotland's loftiest mountains. Miss Foster and Mr Linsk were to have danced as guest artists with the Sadler's Wells Theatre Ballet at Edinburgh last night. Miss Foster's place was taken at the last moment by Miss Chaytor. She and Mr Linsk received quite an ovation for their brilliant dancing in the Blue Bird *pas-de-deux*. Miss Chaytor, a former member of the Metropolitan Ballet Company, joined the Wells not long ago." '

'Well?' said Mrs Sordy again. 'I still don't see what it's got to do wi' us.'

'Don't you remember our Harriet?' pursued Mrs Dickson patiently.

'Course I remember your Harriet. What about your Harriet?'

'Well, she went as kennel-maid to them Monkhouses. *That's* the son,' said Mrs Dickson, pointing to the picture below the paragraph. 'Him that's talking to Miss Mariella Foster. Him and Miss Jane Foster – she's the one that had the accident – are cousins. The world's a small place, I allus say.'

'It is an' all,' agreed Mrs Sordy. 'Fancy your girl bein' kennel-maid to a cousin of a bally-what's-its-name!'

'Oh, Harriet's not there now,' put in Mrs Dickson. 'She

give notice a week afore Christmas. Said Lady Monkhouse was a real tartar, and the young man, too. Ordered her about as if he was Lord God Almighty, and Lady Monkhouse tret our Harriet like as if she was the dust under her feet. Didn't suit our Harriet, that didn't! She's with the MacFarlanes at Bridgend now. He's the veterinary. Harriet says they're real nice folk. I had a letter from her yesterday. Mind you, she had nawt agin Miss Mariella or Miss Jane. Said they was reel ladies – ever so kind and considerate. Harriet says it's goin' around that Mr Nigel is about to get engaged to Miss Mariella, but our Harriet says she hopes Miss Mariella's got more sense than to marry the likes of him!'

'Look, Mam – it says "more pi'tchers on the back page",' shrilled Lily, seizing the paper.

'Give over, Lily!' ordered Mrs Sordy. 'And D'reen, too. You'll tear it, you will! Our Ella can't get her nose in, poor little thing.'

As for Ella, she was staring at the picture of Jane Foster, ballerina of the Sadler's Wells Ballet, her large, dark eyes as round as saucers. She said nothing, but she thought that Miss Jane Foster was the most lovely thing she had ever seen.

'Seems funny to me,' said Mrs Sordy, looking at the photograph with her head on one side, 'standin' on one leg like a stork!'

'Oh, it's all like that nowadays, dear,' said Mrs Dickson, who had seen what she called 'reel bally' on television several times. 'It's wonderful, I always think, how they can stand on the tips of their toes all the time, and never fall over!'

Chapter 3

Rehearsal

No amount of luck alone ever made a ballet dancer, but there's no denying the fact that a bit of luck can do an awful lot to help! Take the case of Ella Sordy, for instance. If it hadn't been for an epidemic of flu, she might never have been heard of. I mean, of course, in the dancing sphere. When Miss Martin promised to lend her friend, Ruth Fisher, a ballet student to coach the children in their dances for the pantomime, she hadn't bargained for the whole lot of them going down with flu.

'I shall just have to go over to Blackheath myself,' she said to her second-in-command, a willowy young lady who was responsible for the ballroom dancing. 'There's nothing else for it.'

'Frightful bore!' remarked the willowy young lady sympathetically.

'Oh, no, I didn't mean that,' Mary Martin said truthfully. And it was a fact – she never *was* bored when taking a class, which doubtless accounted for her success as a teacher. There was always *something* to bring out in the children, and a new class was especially exciting. It was rather like a lucky dip! You never knew what you might pull out of it! Mary Martin never forgot the fact that many Sadler's Wells dancers – soloists among them – had begun their ballet training in her big Newcastle studio. Why, she had even helped towards training Veronica Weston herself!

The fact that most of the Blackheath children had never had a dancing lesson in their lives didn't dismay Mary

Martin. On the contrary, she preferred children to come to her that way. Then there were no faults, due to bad teaching, to correct. The only chidren who caused a furrow to appear on her smooth, round forehead were those who were 'ever so good at tap', or 'ever so cute at musical comedy', or 'just like Margot Fonteyn'. She didn't like the precocious type! As she waited patiently for Ruth Fisher to explain to the assembled pantomime cast what the panto-mime was all about, she picked out Rosie Proud as the only child who was beyond the help of man – or even Mary Martin!

'No, I couldn't do anything with Rosie,' she thought, as she watched the child self-consciously showing off. 'The others are bad, it's true; as far as I can see, there isn't a naturally graceful child among the lot of them, but still – I *might* improve them. Who knows?' She began to teach them.

'Miss Fisher has just told you all that this first scene is about,' she began. 'The main characters are Cinderella's Ugly Sisters, Cinderella's Stepmother, the King, and a crowd of courtiers. Now for the Ugly Sisters – Lily and Doreen Sordy, I think Miss Fisher said. Come over here the two of you. Now, Doreen' (addressing the bigger of the two giggling, blushing girls), 'you're supposed to be dressed in wonderful clothes, so you must show them off. Listen to the music' (she nodded to Ruth who started the gramo-phone). 'It's Elgar's "Pomp and Circumstance". Now, imagine you're very grand. Come along, Lily – let me see you walk – *proudly*, as if you had a long, heavy train behind you. Swing it round you, like this when you reach poor Cinderella. No, no! Don't just walk as if you were going to the shop round the corner to buy a pound of sausages for your mother! Walk as if you were a noble lady – *very* proud, *very* haughty! Behave as if you could hardly bear even to *speak* to Cinderella, crouched in the cinders there.

Imagine you are a peacock, and *strut!* . . . Now you, Doreen. Oh, I know you haven't actually got a train attached to your shoulders, but can't you *pretend* you have?'

But this is what the Blackheath children seemed incapable of doing. They dealt in facts, and facts only. The word 'make-believe' was strange to them – with people watching, anyway. Lily might play at 'houses', and Doreen might be the 'doctor', but not with a couple of grown-ups looking on! As for peacocks – they'd never seen one!

'All right,' said Miss Martin, 'it will get better in time. Now, Cinderella, you must get up from among the cinders and curtsy – so – to your sisters because you are so much younger than they are. So very much humbler; so very much in awe of them.' Although Miss Martin was middle-aged, her every movement was graceful. She swept a curtsy to the Ugly Sisters that made the onlookers draw in their breaths in admiration.

Ella got up from her 'cinders' (a pile of exercise-books) and Mary Martin's heart missed a beat. Here it was – the thing she was always on the look-out for – a child full of natural grace; a child so expressive that every emotion showed in her plain little face, a child whose inmost thoughts were mirrored in her large, dark eyes, like cloud-shadows passing over a lake. Why, even her hands were expressive, and such hands! Mary Martin could hardly believe her eyes. Tiny, thin, with the delicate bones showing through the fine skin – they were the sort of hands that every ballet dancer dreams of. Just as a surgeon must possess strong, sensitive fingers, so must a ballerina possess hands capable of expressing her emotions. A dancer's hands are nearly as important to her as a musician's are to him. Many a dancer has remained in the *corps de ballet* because nature unkindly endowed her with podgy hands!

Miss Martin watched Ella Sordy living her part as the little drudge, watched her walking, watched her portray the thoughts of the poor downtrodden child when spurned by her elder sisters, and knew that she was watching a dancer. Of course, she might never actually *become* a dancer. That is where luck, chance, opportunity – call it what you will – comes in. But to Mary Martin, with all her many years' experience, there was no mistaking it. Ella Sordy, although she hadn't yet learned a step, was a natural, born dancer!

'Now you must curtsy to your sisters,' said Miss Martin. 'This is how you do it. Step to the side – like this – put the other foot behind, and sink down. Watch me!' Once again Mary Martin performed that incredibly graceful curtsy.

Poor Ella! Faced with so unfamiliar and unnatural a thing as a curtsy, her grace vanished. Her legs tied themselves up in knots, and she fell flat!

'It's always so,' thought Miss Martin imperturbably. 'If she learns ballet she'll lose all her lovely grace for a time. But it will come back, and she will be exquisite to watch! In fact, she's lovely to watch now.' As she patiently coached Lily, D'reen, Mabel, Susie and Annie, she held little Ella Sordy in the corner of her eye. It was difficult *not* to watch her, as Ruth Fisher had already discovered when she had stood at one of the long class-room windows when the children were out at play. Every movement of the tiny, exquisite body was so beautiful to behold that it didn't matter a jot that the child's face was plain and pale and all eyes!

When the rehearsal was over, she called the child to her.

'Ella,' she said. 'That is your name, isn't it?'

'Yes, miss,' said Ella.

'Do you like dancing, Ella?'

You might have expected Ella to answer rapturously: 'Oo! *Yes*, miss!' But if so, you would be disappointed.

'No, miss,' she said promptly.

Miss Martin was taken aback. Now here was a puzzle.

'You don't like dancing?' she pursued. 'Now that is very strange, because I thought, when I was watching you just now, that you were loving it.'

'Oh, *that*, miss? You mean the pantomime? I didn't know *that* was dancin'. I thought you meant what Rosie Proud does. Like this' – she tapped with her feet and gesticulated with her hands.

'Well, that is *one* sort of dancing, it's true,' said Miss Martin, 'and sometimes – when performed by a master, like, say, Fred Astaire, it can be very exciting to watch. But I didn't really mean tap-dancing. I meant ballet – *this* sort of dancing.' She pulled a copy of the *Ballet Weekly* out of her attaché-case and opened it at a picture. 'Veronica Weston as Odette in *Lac Des Cygnes*.'

Ella studied the picture silently. Then she gave a little sigh.

'Why the sigh?' questioned Miss Martin.

'She's that luver-ly,' said Ella.

That night Mrs Sordy heard all about Our Ella and her goings-on.

'Answered the teacher back ever so pat!' giggled Lily. 'Said she didna like dancin'! And fell down flat in the curtsy. Everyone fair died of laughin'! Our Ella's a reel sketch!'

'Well, you'd best get yourselves to bed,' said Mrs Sordy, 'or you'll all be late for school the mornin'. Where did you say our Ella was?'

'She's down the bottom of the street lookin' at the heaps.'

'Lookin' at the heaps? Whatever for?' demanded Mrs Sordy.

'They're tippin',' said Lily. 'You know what our Ella is when they're tippin'.'

At the bottom of Pit Street Ella stood, still as under a

spell. In front of her, hunched against the skyline, rose a range of round, black mountains, and, as she watched, a fiery avalanche poured down the side of the nearest one. The whole countryside was lit up by the lurid glare. For a few seconds it remained so. No one except Ella even so much as glanced up at the familiar sight, but to her it was something wonderful and beautiful – even if she *had* seen it dozens and dozens of times before.

As the glare faded, she turned and walked slowly up the street towards 113, where a cracked mug of cocoa, a doorstep of bread and jam, and a bed, sandwiched in between Lily and D'reen, awaited her.

Chapter 4

Ballet comes to Blackheath

Mary Martin had devoted thirty-odd years of her life to ballet. Ever since she was seventeen, and had given up all thought of being a dancer herself, she had striven to pass on her love of the art to other people.

'But why *didn't* you dance yourself, Mary?' was often asked of her.

'I hadn't the necessary perfection of body,' was her answer. 'I should perhaps have reached the *corps de ballet* – if I was lucky – and then only in a third-rate company. The principal companies demand physical perfection even in the *corps de ballet*!'

'But what an awful waste of talent,' the unthinking would say.

Waste of talent? Mary Martin looked round her crowded studios, and thought of the dancers she had given (and would give) to Sadler's Wells and other leading companies; of the number of first-rate dancing teachers she had trained; of the grace and assurance she had bestowed upon countless gawky teenagers, and she smiled wisely. She was a very generous and unselfish person at heart. You might have thought she would have been jealous when her pupils achieved something she had wished for in her own youth – fame behind the footlights – but Mary Martin was content to know she had helped them to get there; that but for her sensitive mind, her devotion to the art, and above all, her infinite patience, these dancers might never have been heard of. More than that, she loved teaching for its own sake.

She loved to watch a child learn to express itself by means of her beloved art. It was like watching a flower unfold in the warmth of the sun. When she saw a child like Ella Sordy . . .

Yes, Ella Sordy. Ella was most certainly at the root of the Blackheath ballet class. Mary Martin couldn't forget the child. Although she probably didn't realize it herself, it was the idea that perhaps Ella Sordy might be there that she suggested to one of her ballet students – a girl, June Robinson by name – that she should start a ballet class in Blackheath.

June wasn't very enthusiastic. After all, who *would* be enthusiastic at the thought of teaching fifty or sixty unruly, untaught children in a colliery village? They'd be shockingly badly behaved, in all probability. As a matter of fact, they weren't nearly as unruly or as badly behaved as some of the children in the Newcastle class who should have known better, but June wasn't to know that.

'Oh, but Miss Martin – do you think—' she began.

Miss Martin cut her short.

'Quite a lot of the children have been asking for a class,' she said. 'The success of the pantomime last month has given them a taste for ballet, and we must foster it. It's our job! Besides, who knows what talent we might find there? Anyhow, it will be good practice for you, June, if you intend to have a school of your own some day.'

'OK, Miss Martin,' said June cheerfully. She was a big, good-tempered girl and she loved her chosen career already. 'When do you want the class to start?'

'As soon as possible, dear,' said Miss Martin. 'I shall go over there myself and see about a hall – there's one in connection with the church, I think, that would do nicely. If I can get the names of about a dozen children, that will be enough for you to start on. There will be a pianist to find, as well. I shall go over to Blackheath on Monday and

27

see what I can do.'

And over she went. Gentle and patient she certainly was, but she was tenacious, too. When she made up her mind, there was no stopping her! She was casting her net for a certain fish, and she was making certain that the fish got caught. She was leaving nothing to chance! She even went so far as to park her little car outside the school gates at half-past three, and offer the three Sordy children a lift down to their home in the Old Village.

'I want to see your mother,' she said. 'Jump in!'

The Sordys jumped in, and Mary Martin noticed how gracefully Ella did it! She also noticed once again the child's exquisite and expressive hands. She looked down at her feet, but all she could see were two small, strong, black, badly fitting shoes that made her wince. Who knew what harm those great, hobnailed things were doing to the delicate bones they compressed!

'I'll tell me mam you wants to see 'er,' shrilled Lily, as the car drew up at number 113. 'Mam! Mam! There's a lady to see yer!'

Mrs Sordy wasn't very forthcoming. She stood in the doorway, arms akimbo, and looked Miss Martin up and down.

'What was you wantin'?' she said at length, while Lily and D'reen hovered in the background expectantly.

Mary Martin explained her errand, and when Mrs Sordy realized that her visitor wasn't the 'District Lady', or someone begging for the church, she asked her to come into the Room. This wasn't the comfortable living-room with the steel fender and the Royal Family, but a smaller and neater room at the back which was kept for Weddings, Funerals, and Special Occasions. There was a black and shiny horsehair sofa that had belonged to Mrs Sordy's mother, and family photographs in green plush frames, and a piano that made a sweet jangly sound if you had the temerity to play upon it. Its strings were decently hidden

28

behind a pleated green silk front.

Miss Martin, perched on the edge of the slippery sofa, unfolded her plan of a ballet class in Blackheath, and Mrs Sordy, sitting stiffly in a chair opposite, listened politely.

'It would only cost twenty pence a class for each child,' said Miss Martin. 'At first the class would be run at a loss—'

'Then why start it, for goodness sake?' demanded Mrs Sordy. 'I don't hold wi' running things at a loss.'

Miss Martin sighed. It was hard to explain.

'Simply because Blackheath is a colliery village, miles and miles from anywhere, doesn't mean that its children should be deprived of the pleasures – the pleasures—' She began to falter under Mrs Sordy's cold, grey-eyed gaze. But she'd hit the right note. The very thought of Our Ella, Our D'reen, not to mention Our Lily (ever Mrs Sordy's favourite) being deprived of *anything* couldn't be borne.

'You're right there,' said Mrs Sordy. 'No more they should! But twenty pence a class! We're nobbut poor folk, miss – I forget what you said your name was—'

'Martin,' supplied her visitor.

'There's three on 'em, Miss Martin,' went on Mrs Sordy. 'That's sixty pence a week. It's a bit stiff, if you see what I mean – with their Dad on Disability. I might manage the twenty pence for *one* of 'em.'

'I *was* going to suggest I took the youngest child free,' said Mary Martin hopefully. But alas! She rejoiced too soon!

'That's reel good of you, I'm sure,' said Mrs Sordy. 'Our Lily—'

'I really should have said the *smallest*,' put in Miss Martin with a quick wit, born of sheer desperation. How was she to know that Ella, although much the smallest of the Sordys, was the eldest of the three! 'That is, Ella.'

'Well!' said Mrs Sordy. 'Fancy that! I *was* going to suggest Our Lily came free and Our D'reen on the twenty

29

pence, but if you reely wants a plain little thing like Our Ella – well, it's *your* funeral, Miss er—'

'Martin,' said Mary once more. 'Well, that's settled, then. The class will begin in a week's time – next Thursday – in the Church Hall. I shall expect Lily with her twenty pence, and Ella can come free.'

'I believe I'd have *paid* that woman to let the child come,' she thought fiercely as she drove away under the curious gaze of most of the inhabitants of Pit Street, hidden behind their window curtains. 'How on earth did a big, square-faced, raw-boned, insensitive woman like that manage to have a child like Ella? It's incomprehensible!'

Mary Martin, you see, knew nothing at all about the Sordy family history.

The Blackheath Ballet School (as it now called itself) grew in numbers and in popularity. June Robinson had a strong and willing personality. She was kind and patient, and she could keep order. She was, in fact, a born teacher. Over and above the members of Ruth Fisher's famous panto-mime, there were ten children from the New Estate, including Rosie Proud, whose mother wouldn't allow her darling to be left out of anything. Last but not least, there was Elizabeth Ann Green to 'lend tone' to the proceedings (this was how her mother put it to the dancing mistress). So now there were twenty children of assorted ages and sizes, diligently practising traditional ballet exercises in the church hall. Two long rows of chairs did duty for *barres*, and all down Coronation Road (as the latest street in the new housing estate was called) you could hear Miss Robinson's commands: 'One-and-two-and-three-and-four-and – stretch the insteps, children! – turn out from the thighs, not only from the knees – close in third position – *dégagé* – now on the other side. Begin! – one-and-two-and-three-and . . .' just as you could hear the same words in Sadler's

Wells School itself!

It was amazing how those children progressed! Even Our Lily began to look less angular, and Rosie Proud less precocious. Elizabeth Ann's pink hair ribbon bobbed less stiffly, as she tried to follow her teacher's command to 'watch your hands in the *ports des bras* movements, darling'. As for Ella Sordy. . .

'I don't believe that child's true!' said June Robinson to Miss Fisher when they met in the latter's lodging for a cup of tea after the class. 'She's there practising before the class begins, and she stays behind to practise afterwards. I literally have to hoof the kid out! And then I'll bet a hundred to one she comes back after I've safely gone! She's an infant prodigy all right!'

'But is she really *good?*' pursued Ruth. Having chosen Ella for the pantomime, she took a proprietary interest in her. It was as though she had 'discovered' her.

'Good?' echoed June. 'She's more than good. She's – oh, *wait* till Mary sees her! I'm keeping her dark just now, but just you wait! It's our Summer Show, and Mary wants some kids from this class to be in it – always provided they can get their own costumes. They're very easy – the costumes, I mean. Navy blue tights and white blouses, mostly. She wants a dance that will fit into her Fairy-tale Book scene, so I thought Ella Sordy could do her Cinderella dance out of your pantomime, Ruth, if you'll agree. *That's* when I'm going to spring Ella on Mary Martin!'

'Of course you can include the dance in your show,' said Ruth. 'But as a matter of fact,' she added thoughtfully, 'I shouldn't be surprised if Mary hasn't had her eye on Ella all along. She watched her all the time she was dancing in *Cinderella*, I noticed particularly. Of course, it *may* have been just because she *was* Cinderella, but somehow I don't think so. I think she'd have watched Ella even if she'd been a page boy, or the castle cat!'

'You may be right,' agreed June. 'She's a deep one is our dear Mary! Now I remember, she *did* tell me to let Ella in free because the Sordys couldn't afford to pay for three kids. I thought it was very decent of her, but it may have been more than that. . . Look, Ruth, angel – will you be a sport and give it out in school tomorrow, about the show. I ought to have told them today, but I forgot. Impress upon them about the dresses, will you! We can't be responsible for twenty lots of tights and blouses! Thanks awfully, Ruth! I must dash! My bus is in five minutes. Bye-bye!'

The next day, when Miss Fisher made the announcement about the forthcoming Summer Show, there was a twitter of excitement among the members of the ballet class.

'You're to do your limbering-up exercises,' explained Ruth, 'and there was something else – I'm not quite sure what, but Miss Robinson will be telling you about it next Thursday. Oh, and I was to tell you all to explain to your mothers that if you want to be in the show you *must* provide your own costumes. They're very simple – just black or navy blue tights and white blouses. I expect most of you have got them already—'

'Please, miss, where is the show to be?' asked Rosie Proud.

'In the Theatre Royal, Newcastle,' answered Miss Fisher. 'It's to be a matinée – that's in the afternoon, you know, and the proceeds are for the RSPCA.'

There was an awed chorus of 'oos', and 'ahs'. A real theatre!

'Oh yes, and I nearly forgot a most important thing – Miss Martin wants Ella Sordy to do Cinderella's dance out of our pantomime – the one with the broomstick, remember? Well, she is going to include that dance in her "Characters out of Fairyland" scene. Yes, you Ella. You're to wear a new grey and white frock, Ella, with lots of white frills underneath. Aren't you lucky? Aren't you thrilled?'

'Yes, miss,' Ella said dutifully, but when the excitement had died down, she sat staring at the floor, her pale little face even paler than usual. Thrilled? Yes, of course she was thrilled. Who wouldn't be thrilled at the very idea of being in a real ballet show, at a real theatre, and most especially at doing a dance all by herself on a real stage? She knew what the fairy-tale character scene was like, because all the others had been talking about it. There was a huge book at the back of the stage, and all the fairy-tale characters came through it – Jack and Jill, Beauty and the Beast in pairs; Little Miss Muffet all by herself, Jack Horner by himself; the Babes in the Wood, and then – then Cinderella, Ella Sordy. It was so beautiful that she didn't care to think about it because, of course, it was quite, quite impossible. Miss Fisher had told them – had stressed the point – that all the children who wished to be in the show must supply their own costumes. It would be hard enough to get her Mam to buy the tights and blouses for herself and Lily. As for a fabulous ballet dress of grey and white with frills underneath – there wasn't a hope! Ella knew that quite well. It wasn't that Me Mam was harder than anybody else's mam under the same circumstances. The fact was, money was extremely short in the Sordy family.

That night, when Lily broached the subject, Mrs Sordy promised to do what she could about the tights and blouses.

'But not the other fal-lals! What does the woman think I'm made of? 'Sides, our Lily ain't havin' no chiffon dress, and if *she* ain't, there isn't no reason why you should. The very idea!' As we have said before, Our Mam favoured Lily, possibly because she was the youngest of the family. Lily hadn't benefited by this favouritism, either. She was, speaking candidly, fast becoming a 'proper little brat', as Mrs Dickson put it.

Ella didn't make a scene as the more spoilt Lily would

certainly have done. She didn't fling herself on her bed and cry herself to sleep. For one thing, it's difficult to fling yourself on a bed you share with two other people, and if you cried, Lily would soon tell you to 'shut up, or I'll give you what for!'

Ella lay quite still, thinking about her Cinderella dance, and doing, in her mind, all the much-loved steps and actions. She couldn't perform the dance in public, it is true, but no one could stop her doing it in her imagination.

Then she had an idea. Mr Roebottom, the vicar, had once taken a children's service in connection with the Sunday School, and he had said: 'If you want anything passionately, go to church and ask God for it, and if it is good for you to have this thing, then be sure He will give it to you. But do not be disappointed if God does not grant your wish, because, you see, it may *not* be good for you. It is a fact, we do not always know what is good for us, and what is bad. You must not regard God as a sort of magic wishbone!'

Surely, thought Ella, God couldn't mind her asking Him for a frilly dress to dance her Cinderella dance in? She determined to try that very next Sunday.

Chapter 5

The Sunday School

Mrs Roebottom, the vicar's wife, took the Sunday School. She was an excessively thin woman with greying hair and very blue eyes. Mrs Roebottom's clothes were very easy to describe because they were always the same. In winter she wore an old, brown tweed coat over a brown tweed suit, topped by a brown felt riding-hat. In summer, the coat was discarded and the vicar's wife appeared in the suit alone. The hat remained the same. The reason for this conservative choice in clothes wasn't, as you might think, lack of imagination, but lack of money.

There were a great many children in the Blackheath Sunday School. They didn't go because they wanted to, but because they were driven there by parents who wanted a bit of peace and quiet on Sundays. There were the exceptions, of course. Ella Sordy, for instance, who went willingly, because the Bible stories were 'that luver-ly', and she liked to look at the stained-glass windows in the church (especially the one with Christ and the little children, and the other one depicting an angel with great white wings), and she liked the sound of the organ when Mrs Roebottom played the hymns upon it. It was really only a harmonium of very ancient make, but to Ella Sordy it sounded like music from heaven. Besides these things, Ella liked Mrs Roebottom's blue eyes, and the way they lit up when she smiled and, most of all, she liked the way she spoke. The vicar's wife came from a remote manse, in a village called Inverochan, on the west coast of Scotland, and she had a lovely soft, lilting, Highland Scottish voice.

On this particular Sunday, however – the Sunday after little Ella Sordy had made up her mind to ask the help of her Maker – Mrs Roebottom was laid up with a heavy cold, so her place as Sunday School teacher was taken by her son, Timothy, a large, loose-limbed youth of eighteen, who was in his last year at his public school, and was home for his half-term weekend.

During the Christmas holidays Timothy had taken a temporary job sorting letters at the general post office in Newcastle. With his salary, together with two cheques – Christmas presents from an adoring maiden aunt and a conscientious godfather respectively – he had managed to buy an ancient car – a vehicle so old that in another year or two it would qualify as a museum piece! It was a sports model, painted by Timothy himself a dashing scarlet. Its convertible top, patched with pieces of an old ground-sheet by the ever-resourceful Timothy, flapped in the wind, so that, together with the awesome noise made by its engine, it sounded exactly like an infuriated prehistoric dragon about to take flight!

Where Timothy Roebottom got the necessary petrol from to run his car, and the money for his insurance and road tax, nobody knew, but vicars' sons are ever-resourceful, and Timothy always seemed to have the wherewithal to run his 'old bus'. Judging by the clouds of smoke coming out of the exhaust, Blackheath said they suspected he raided his mother's oil supply!

The Vicarage was situated in the Old Village. It consisted of a couple of pit cottages knocked into one. Outside, it presented a murky exterior of dirty yellow bricks, speckled with grime. Inside, its small, square rooms had an aspect of decayed gentility. Mrs Roebottom had been a Scottish minister's daughter, and her father had been out in India for some years, and had brought home with him many curios, all of which had, in the course of time, descended to his only daughter. Carved ivory and ebony elephants stood on the painted mantelshelf in the sitting-room. Indian rugs, so threadbare that they no longer had any patterns, covered the polished floor which was tilted at a peculiar angle through subsidence due to colliery 'workings' underneath. The cracked walls were ornamented by a collection of curious daggers and other weapons and a prayer-rug which glowed out of the darkness with an amazing beauty. A crude blue and red native jug held a great bush of pampas grass in one corner, while in another stood a little bamboo table with an old Chinese mandarin upon it, for ever grimacing hideously, and nodding his head whenever anyone walked over the rickety floor.

The church was down in the Old Village, too, but since most of the people had been moved into the council houses up in the New Estate, a small daughter church had been built there, half a mile away, complete with a church hall, and it was here that most of the church activities of Blackheath took place, including the Sunday School.

To watch Timothy Roebottom coax his six-foot frame out of his pint-size car was something worth watching! First, out came his long legs, clad in a pair of thread-bare tweeds if it was winter, or even more threadbare jeans if it was summer. After this, out would come two enormous paws – Timothy's hands, engulfed in ancient sheepskin mitts. Lastly, the rest of Timothy – patched tweed jacket, topped by an ex-navy duffel coat if it were cold, and above it a shock head of fair, curly hair. The entire Sunday School watched this exciting proceeding from out of the vestry windows, though, when Timothy finally strode into the church, they were all in their seats as meek as mice!

It was well known to the whole Sunday School that the vicar's son had only one Bible story he knew really well. Whenever he took the class for his mother, out it came.

They waited expectantly.

'I'm going to tell you a story,' began Timothy.

'Yes, miss.' The children nudged each other, and one or two giggled. 'Which one, miss?'

'The one about the loaves and fishes,' announced Timothy and wondered why the class was suddenly convulsed. 'It's nothing to giggle about, you girls! It's not at all funny, you chaps! It's a miracle. What is a miracle, by the way?'

Up shot a forest of hands.

'Please, miss – I know!' 'I know, miss!' 'Ask me, miss!' 'Me, miss! No, don't ask him, miss – he's only being daft! Ask me! . . .'

'Shut up, all of you!' ordered Timothy. 'You, Rosie. What is a miracle?'

'A miracle is summat flying over the church steeple,' said Rosie triumphantly. 'You telt us that last time.'

'Like a flying saucer!' said a voice from one of the back rows. George Stobbs trying to be funny, thought Timothy. He turned to Rosie.

'I didn't say that at all,' he declared. 'I said that if *you* were to fly over the church steeple it would be a miracle. If a bird flew over, it wouldn't.'

'Why wouldn't it?'

'Because it's natural for a bird to fly. It isn't natural for you to fly.'

'Why isn't it?'

'Oh, shut up!' said Timothy again. He knew perfectly well they were just baiting him. 'Can anyone tell me of another miracle?'

'Yes, miss. Swimming down the river and not bein' drownded.'

'*No*, Lily – not swimming. *Walking*. Walking down the river.'

'Please, miss, you walks on a road – not on a river.'

'I know you do – that's the whole point,' exclaimed poor Timothy. 'Oh, gosh! How can I explain? Well, George? Can *you* tell me what would be a miracle?'

'I can and all!' said George, a lout of fourteen, with a shock of red hair, freckles, and a large, coarse mouth. 'It'd be a miracle if you was to tell us a fresh story, Timothy Roebottom! We's heard that'n ower many times!'

'It would be a miracle if you would learn to keep a civil tongue in your head!' retorted Timothy. Inwardly he seethed with fury.

Meanwhile the Sunday School tittered. They considered that Timothy Roebottom, with his public-school accent, was a snob. What about his car, for one thing. Why should *he* own a car? He was only the parson's son. Their dads got better paid than the vicar. Anyway, he hadn't yet left school! Car, indeed! To be fair, they didn't know he had worked for the money and bought the car himself, but even if they had, it is doubtful whether it would have made a great deal of difference. Jealousy is an unreasoning thing.

The hymn-singing went off better than the story. Children like singing at any time, and one or two badly behaved boys, like George Stobbs, weren't going to stop them. They sang 'All Things Bright and Beautiful' at the top of their voices, and although there might not be any real music in it, they made a goodly noise that effectively drowned George and his cronies whispering in the back pews.

'OK,' said Timothy, after the last prayer. 'You can shove off now.'

The class shoved off, pushing and cuffing each other, and shouting at the top of their voices.

'Afraid I shouldn't cut much ice as a schoolmaster!' said Timothy ruefully to himself, as the last of the yelling, struggling crowd disappeared out of the church gates. 'But, of course, one's got no hold over them. George Stobbs can cuff young Willie Pratt and sock him on the jaw. Alfie

Wood can kick Ernie Robinson into the ditch and trample on him, and none of the parents would turn a hair. But if *I* gave George "one for himself", the whole place – mams, dads, uncles, aunts, the whole bag of tricks – would be out for my blood, and I'd be had up in court for assault! They're like a family. They squabble amongst themselves, but let anybody else . . . Gosh! Look at the church! What a frightful mess! . . .'

The Sunday School had taken advantage of Timothy's ignorance, and had left their hymn books and hassocks in a wild state of disorder, a thing they would never have dared to do had the vicar's wife been present. Soft-voiced Mrs Roebottom might be, but she could keep order. Even George Stobbs sat silent (if rebellious) in the back pew, when Mrs Roebottom explained the Bible story for the day.

In disgust Timothy began to straighten things up. The pews were littered with hymn books lying, spread-eagled, with leaves crumpled, and, in some cases, torn. Some of them (those in the back pews) had rude faces drawn on the fly-leaves, and even ruder remarks written on the margins. George and his cronies had certainly been having a field day! Hassocks lay about in drunken disorder. Timothy hung them up on their hooks, and straightened the cushions in the pews. He was just about to leave the church with a sigh of thankfulness, and had, in fact, reached the door, when a slight sound made him turn. He stopped with his hand on the latch and listened. Yes, there it was again – a sound like a smothered sob. Someone was still in the church!

He closed the door again softly and strode back up the aisle and into the sanctuary. It was dark up there, but he could see the shadowy figure of a child kneeling up beside the altar rails. 'Hullo,' said Timothy. 'Who is that? What are you doing there?'

The kneeling figure looked round, and a pair of startled

dark eyes looked into his own blue ones. He recognized the child as the pale little girl who listened to his words so attentively and politely that he had instinctively addressed most of his remarks about loaves and fishes to her.

'What's up?' he asked. 'Are you in trouble?'

'Oh, yes, miss,' said the girl in a whisper.

The young man felt a rush of pity for the forlorn child. She was so pale, so very plain, so obviously in the depths of woe. He sat down on the step beside her.

'Care to tell me,' he asked her, 'or would you rather not?'

'I was just praying about it,' said Ella. 'The vicar said if God thought a thing was good for you, He might give it to you. Do you think God would help us about me dress?'

Timothy looked down at her, surprised. A dress? Now what on earth did she want a dress for? She didn't look *that* sort of a kid – the sort craving for fine clothes already. Why, she could only be about ten!

'A dress?' he repeated. 'What sort of a dress? You mean a *party* dress?'

'Oh, *no*, miss,' said Ella. 'I means a ballet dress.' (She had learned to pronounce the word correctly by this time.) And then out it all came. Into Timothy Roebottom's ears she poured the story of the pantomime, *Cinderella*, her lovely dance, the beautiful grey and white costume with the frills underneath, the forthcoming show. . .

'But you see, miss,' she concluded, 'we all has to provide our own dresses. And you couldn't expect me Mam to give us one, could you? She's that hard up, is me Mam, since me Dad took ill.'

'Money troubles again!' thought Timothy Roebottom, with a sigh of understanding. 'Filthy lucre! The problems of ways and means!' He knew all about that, did the vicar's son! 'Fellow feeling makes us wondrous kind' as the saying goes.

'Something must be done,' he said aloud. 'Where there's

41

a will there's a way! I believe your prayer has been answered, kid. God usually does it through a third person, you know. Perhaps He sent me here today to lend a hand. Anyway, I have an idea!'

'Oh, miss!' said Ella. 'Do you mean you know where I could get a ballet dress?' Her dark eyes glowed out of her pale face.

'Good Lord!' thought Timothy. 'I thought she was plain! Why, she's almost pretty!'

'I won't promise,' he answered cautiously, 'but, as I said, I've got an idea. Come along, kid.' He took her by the hand, and they left the church, side by side.

'Mind the old bone-shaker?' he inquired when they reached the church gate. He nodded proudly at the evil-looking monster squatting on the square of grass.

'You mean I'm to come with you, miss – in your car?' said Ella.

'That's the idea,' said Timothy, opening the door for her, and then squeezing himself behind the steering wheel on the other side. 'It's a goodish way to where the lady I have in mind lives.'

Ella had sometimes ridden in Our Sid's new car, with its imitation leather seats and its glitter of chromium, but she liked this little car better, though it did rattle and emit clouds of blue smoke. For one thing, it had seats of real leather (Timothy pointed this out proudly as they went), and for another, her knight-errant was driving it! She sat there in a dream of happiness. Her trust in him was implicit. God had answered her prayer and had sent Timothy Roebottom to her! She stole a glance at him and noted his fair, curly hair and intent boyish profile. Yes, he was a perfect knight-errant. No, on second thoughts, he was more like the Prince in *Cinderella!*

'Well now, Miss Jones, do you think you could help us

42

out?' asked Timothy, when he had introduced Ella, and had explained the position. 'It must be a grey ballet-length dress – that right, kid? – with frilly thingumibobs underneath, something like *Giselle* in the first act.' (Timothy was a great admirer of ballet, and frequented the gallery whenever the ballet came to Newcastle.)

Gweneth Jones nodded thoughtfully. She was a dressmaker, and a bit of an artist as well. Most dressmakers are.

'What sort of material do you want?' she asked.

'We leave that to you, Gweneth,' said Timothy. 'Don't we, Ella?'

'I'll do my very best,' promised Miss Jones. Something in the little girl's face had touched her, too. 'I'll just take her measurements, and she can look in for a fitting next Saturday. Will that do?' She turned to Ella.

'It will that, miss!' said Ella, with shining eyes. 'And *thank* you ever so, miss!' Then her face fell. 'Oh, but, miss – the money for the material – I haven't got none, and me Mam—'

'That's all right,' Timothy put in hurriedly. 'Miss Jones has lots of bits and pieces of stuff left over from other people's clothes that will cover a scrap like you. Haven't you, Gwen?' His hand stole into his pocket and came out again with a ten pound note hidden in the palm. Unseen by Ella he passed it silently to the dressmaker and put a finger to his lips. 'Haven't you, Gweneth?'

'Lots of lovely bits,' said Miss Jones. 'I promise you it will be the dress of dresses! A work of art!'

Timothy took Ella home in his little car, and the inhabitants of Pit Street stared from behind their curtains. The vicar's son giving lifts to the Sordy kid. What next!

'I think, if I were you, I should keep this dress under your hat,' advised Timothy, as the car drew up with a screeching of brakes at number 113. 'Say nothing about it,

43

I mean. It might be better. You'll remember Miss Jones's address. Mount Pleasant – number 56. I'd take you up there in the old bus, but I'll be back at school. Anyway, I'm going to lay her up for a bit.'

'Why, miss?' asked Ella.

'Oh – just ways and means,' said Timothy airily. 'Ways and means, you know. Petrol and so forth. So long, kid!'

He squeezed back into his car, the engine roared, the gears clashed, the car spat fire and smoke, and he was gone. It was rather like the genie in *Aladdin,* thought Ella, as she watched him turn the corner at the bottom of Pit Street, and the sound of his going died away. She stood there for a moment quite still, lost in thought.

'*Ella!*' shouted a voice from inside the house – Me Mam's voice. '*Ella!* Whatever are you doing standing there like a stuck pig! Don't you want no tea?'

Ella jumped. Her thoughts had indeed been miles away. She had been thinking of Miss Jones and the ballet dress, of her dance, and the way the frills would billow and swirl when she turned a pirouette (yes, she'd learned how to do a pirouette – just one turn – at the last ballet class and she'd been practising ever since!) of Timothy Roebottom and his fair curls – like Sir Galahad in the poetry book she had got out of the school library once.

'Coming, Mam!' she called back.

Fortunately for Ella the Sordys had a visitor and were consequently far too busy to ask a lot of awkward questions. The visitor was Mrs Dickson from next door, and she stood by the table, a wet dishcloth in her hands, and steam rising from her thin, red arms. 'He' (meaning Mr Dickson, her husband) had just come in with the Sunday paper, and she'd brought it in to tell her neighbour the news, not even stopping to finish the washing up.

' "Horse Sports at Dewburn in Northumberland," ' she read out, plonking a steaming wet finger on a headline at

44

the top of the front page. 'That's near where our Harriet works. "Mile Over Fences – First, Mr Guy Charlton on Harvester; Second, Mr Nigel Monkhouse on Miss Foster's mare, Jasmine Flower; Third, Miss Jean MacFarlane on Custard Cup." That's our Harriet's young lady. I told you she was with the MacFarlanes of Bridgend, didn't I? . . . Look! Here's a pit'cher of Mr Charlton. Now he's what I call a reel good-lookin' young man! Oh, and there's a pit'cher of Mr Nigel, too . . . "Mr Nigel Monkhouse talking to Miss Mariella Foster in the paddock . . ." '

'Oh, look, Mam!' broke in Ella. 'Look at the lovely ballet pit'cher! It's Veronica Weston, the famous ballet dancer. Miss Robinson told us all about her. What's it say? . . . "News from Sadler's Wells – Miss Veronica Weston, Prima Ballerina Assoluta of the Sadler's Wells Company, was unable to appear at the Gala Performance at Covent Garden last night. A little bird tells us that she is having a baby! Many congratulations, Miss Weston! The ballerina's place was taken by Miss Jane Foster, one of the youngest and newest dancers of the company. The two dancers are seen here in Miss Weston's dressing-room shaking hands before the performance. Further pictures on back page." '

'Quick! Quick! Mam!' begged Ella. 'It says on the back page!'

'Give over pushin', Our Ella!' ordered Mrs Sordy. 'You're gettin' reel rough! There's other folk besides *you* want to get a look in.'

Ella said no more. She would see the paper when the rest of the family had done with it, and anyway, she was far too happy to care whether she saw it or not. She was going to dance at the Mary Martin Summer Show in a real theatre. She had found a fairy prince – one with fair curls and a kind heart. She hoped Miss Mariella Foster would find someone nice, too. Someone a lot nicer than that horrible Nigel Monkhouse.

45

Part Two

Chapter 1

The Monkhouses of Bychester

The Monday after the Horse Sports at Dewburn, Mariella saddled up Lady Jane, and set off for Hordon Castle. She would return Guy's horse, and also call at Bychester Tower for her own Jasmine Flower which she had lent to Nigel. It was fortunate that Hordon wasn't very far from Bychester. All the same, thought Mariella, it would have been a lot more convenient if Nigel had offered to bring Jasmine Flower back himself (Guy had already offered to collect his own mare), but he had rung up Mariella to say that he simply hadn't the time.

'Oh, well, I can pop in and see Ann Musgrave before dinner tonight,' said Mariella to herself. 'It's a lovely day for a ride, and who knows – perhaps Nigel will turn up while I'm there. He might even remember it's the Hunt Ball tonight in the Old Assembly Rooms in Newcastle, and ask me to go with him. He half hinted at it ages ago, and I could just manage it if I took my case along with me and went straight to the station from the dance. How lovely that would be – to have Nigel to see me off! Anyway, I'm pretty sure to get asked to tea, always provided Aunt Phyllis' (she called Nigel's mother 'aunt' out of courtesy), 'is in a good temper!'

Lady Monkhouse was not in a good temper, but Mariella got her longed-for invitation to tea all right. She found Nigel's mother in the stables, as usual, and she hailed Mariella when the latter was quite a long way off.

'Oh, hullo, Mariella! Just the person I wanted to see! Goodall's wretched mother is ill, and Goodall has had to go home to look after her. Really, I don't know what these kennel-maids are coming to. Goodall is the third I've had since Harriet Dickson.'

'Oh!' Mariella didn't know what to say. She had seen Mrs Goodall shopping in Hexham only that morning, but she was far too diplomatic to say so. She suspected that Sheila Goodall, a gentle girl and one who hated scenes, had taken the easiest (if the most cowardly) way of giving Lady Monkhouse notice.

'Yes,' went on Lady Monkhouse, 'it's odd how these people's mothers always fall ill at the most inconvenient times. There is the Tyndale Point-to-Point on Saturday, and all the others coming along during the next few weeks. I told the girl I couldn't possibly give her her wages this week, leaving me without notice like that. Fortunately she went home on the Friday, just before her money was due. It's just a wonder she didn't wait until the Saturday when she'd got it, and then sneak off! Really, the bother I've had with these girls! There was that impertinent chit who told me Nigel had asked her to clean his riding-boots. As if he would! And even if he *had*, what harm would it have done her while we were short of a kitchen-maid, and then to turn round and tell me she hadn't come here to clean my son's boots! Then there was that Watford girl who actually dared to bring her young man here, and give him cups of tea in the harness-room – telling me tales about him missing his bus! And now Goodall. . .' She plied the dandy-brush with such vigour that Polix lifted his hind foot and swished his tail in mild protest.

Mariella's thoughts dwelt on the offending Sheila for a brief moment. She was a very pretty girl, with golden hair cut across her forehead in a straight fringe, and falling in a gleaming 'page boy' to her shoulders. She had a beautiful, lissom figure, and the horses and dogs loved her. On horseback, she looked a perfect picture. Her father was a poor clergyman, and her mother exceedingly delicate, though Mariella was quite sure it wasn't illness that had called Sheila home.

'I expect she was scared to death of Aunt Phyllis,' she thought, 'Aunt Phyllis can be pretty terrifying!'

'Well, now you're here, Mariella, you can give me a hand,' went on Lady Monkhouse. 'Can you stay to tea?. . . Oh, good! There are the hens to feed, as usual, and the eggs to collect. *And* to wash! And there are two stables to muck out, and the kennels to clean—'

'All right, Aunt Phyllis,' said Mariella good-naturedly. She slid from Lady Jane's back, and was about to lead her into the nearest loose-box when Lady Monkhouse stopped her.

'That's a nice mare! Belongs to Charlton of Hordon, doesn't she?'

'Yes, I'm just taking her back,' said Mariella. 'Guy lent her to me for yesterday's Sports.'

'Well, you can leave her here,' said Lady Monkhouse, 'because I've decided to buy her. She's just the mare I've been looking for.'

'But, Aunt Phyllis, I don't think Guy has any idea of selling her,' said Mariella.

Lady Monkhouse regarded her with scorn.

'My dear child, he'll sell all right when he hears the price I'm prepared to pay. Every horse has its price, you know.'

'I don't think Lady Jane has,' Mariella answered. 'I feel pretty sure Guy—'

49

'We shall see, Mariella. We shall see,' said Lady Monkhouse, cutting her short. 'But take her back, of course, if you wish. I can always send over for her tomorrow. I shall ring up Charlton tonight.'

'Yes, I think that would be best, Aunt Phyllis,' said Mariella quietly.

'Well, then, put her in the end loose-box, and let's get on,' said Lady Monkhouse irritably. 'What are you standing there for? You'd better put on Goodall's dungarees. I'll feed the hens – I don't trust anyone with my hens – and you muck out the stables.'

The sitting-room at Bychester was a beautiful room. It was long-shaped, with a rounded end, and had mullioned windows, framed in Virginian creeper, through which you could see the mossy sweep of the Bychester lawns sloping away down to the beech woods. The walls were panelled to within a foot or so of the ceiling. Let into the panelling were paintings of the Monkhouse family – all the people who had lived in this beautiful room, thought Mariella, as she looked up at the picture of the Lady Selina Monkhouse, in a pale grey crinoline gown, with roses in her hair, and hands demurely folded in her lap. At her feet lay a little white dog. She wasn't much like Aunt Phyllis, thought Mariella – except for the dog! She looked as if butter wouldn't melt in her mouth!

The girl's eyes strayed round the rest of the room. The floor was covered with an exquisite but threadbare Persian carpet of a great age. Round the walls were lacquer cabinets, filled with priceless china – delicate cups and saucers with deep, crinkled gold rims and no handles, Crown Derby fruit-bowls with the painted fruit glowing on them as if ready for the picking! There were hand-painted Chinese tea-sets, brought home by the Monkhouse younger sons who had been in the Royal Navy; tall ruby and silver glasses from Venice; porcelain figurines from the Far East. Any one of these things would have brought in a great deal of money at Christie's, but the Monkhouses never thought of selling them. They were part of the Monkhouse heritage, to be handed down to Nigel and his descendants. His wife would have the care of them.

'That will be me – if I marry Nigel,' thought Mariella. 'If he asks me, I should say!'

As for the rest of the room, it was filled with easy chairs and settees in chintz covers, faded white with the sun and much washing, owing to the number of dogs of various kinds that sat upon them. At the moment there were two spaniels and a dachshund that snored loudly and scratched its tummy sleepily when Mariella pushed it along to make room for herself.

The tea was the pale China kind, and the tea-service was English china, with thin cups garlanded with roses, and a great deal of gilt. There were crumpets and hot girdle-scones, fruit cake, and cream cheese.

'I have to attend a meeting of the executive committee of the Federation of Countrywomen this evening in New-castle,' said Lady Monkhouse, spreading cream cheese on a slab of fruitcake, and taking a bite out of it with her large, square, white teeth. She sat on a settee, her green-stockinged legs wide apart, as if she were astride a horse, thought her guest. 'Awful bore, but naturally they expect me to give them a lead. It's about the new lecturers for the panel of speakers. A Mrs Somebody (I forget the woman's name) on ballet, and Rupert Stock – appropriate name, isn't it – on dog breeding. I feel that the ballet is quite unsuitable for these people – they just wouldn't understand it' (privately Mariella wondered if Lady Monkhouse did herself!), 'but I think that Rupert Stock might be quite amusing, don't you? Oh, well – I shall have to go, I suppose, and give the committee the benefit of my advice.

We don't want the Federation to go all highbrow, do we?'

Mariella said nothing. She was thinking that, in her youth, Lady Monkhouse had probably been quite good-looking. Her florid complexion (red-veined, now, through wind and weather and too-good living) had probably been milk and roses. Her blue eyes probably hadn't been as hard then as they were now, and she'd most likely had a comely figure in those far-off days. 'They say, "like mother, like daughter",' thought Mariella. 'I wonder if it applies to sons? Will Nigel turn out like Aunt Phyllis?' She decided that it was impossible. Why, Nigel was the best-looking young man for miles around!

'When are you going back to college?' asked Lady Monkhouse, helping herself to a piece of crumpet, and spreading honey on it. 'Tomorrow?'

'No, tonight,' answered Mariella. 'I'm going up on the midnight train. It's just been a flying visit, you see. We got today off for a mid-term break. I shouldn't have come home if it hadn't been for the Horse Sports, but I just couldn't bear to miss them.'

'You were lucky to have a mount like that mare of Charlton's,' observed Lady Monkhouse. 'You know a thing or two, Mariella – to palm off your old Jas on Nigel so that you could borrow Charlton's Lady Jane. I hand it to you!'

'Oh, but Aunt Phyllis. . .' began Mariella. Then she stopped suddenly. It wasn't easy to explain to Nigel's own mother that Nigel had borrowed Jasmine Flower in the first place, leaving her, Mariella, with no mount at all, and that but for Guy Charlton, who'd come to her rescue at the last moment with his offer of Lady Jane, she wouldn't have been riding in the Sports at all. Fortunately just at this moment, the telephone rang, and Lady Monkhouse went across to the bureau on which it stood to answer it.

'Oh, yes,' Mariella heard her say, 'I got your letter all right. I was outraged by it. Yes, *outraged!* After all these years – and the bill was only eighteen months overdue . . . yes, I shall send you a cheque tomorrow and take my custom elsewhere in the future. *Good*-bye! . . . The very idea!' she added to Mariella, as she put down the receiver. 'Just because I ignored their "account rendered" note, they send me a solicitor's letter, and threaten to bring me into the County court! *Me*, mind you! I should like to see them do it! A little twopenny-ha'penny shop suing Lady Monkhouse of Bychester for a stupid little bill for seventy-five pounds or so! The very idea! Oh, well – as you heard me tell them, I shall take my custom elsewhere, and *they'll* be the losers. I've always been a good customer at Dillings. Spent thousands with them over the last few years. I shall warn all my friends, too, you may be sure. "Don't deal with Dillings," I shall say. "They expect you to pay on the nail, and if you're a day overdue they actually threaten you! There's only one thing to do with people like that – boycott them!" '

Mariella said nothing.

'Remember what I said, Mariella,' repeated Lady Monkhouse. 'Boycott them . . . Mariella, I don't believe you're listening!'

'Oh, yes I am, Aunt Phyllis,' said Mariella. 'You were talking about boycotting people.' Then a thought struck her. Did Aunt Phyllis mean when she, Mariella, was married to Nigel? Could she be meaning that? She stared at Lady Monkhouse, the colour flooding to her cheeks, but Nigel's mother was cutting herself another piece of fruit cake, and it was impossible to tell whether her words had any deep meaning or not. The telephone rang again, and Lady Monkhouse looked up, annoyed.

'That thing, again! I swear I'll have it taken out! Never a minute's peace! Answer it for me, will you, Mariella. It'll be Robert, most likely, wanting to be met somewhere, and me with a "committee" in town and, of course, Goodall not here!'

But it wasn't Sir Robert, Nigel's father. It was Nigel himself. Mariella clutched the edge of the bureau – it was so lovely, such a thrill, just to hear Nigel's voice over the wires.

'Hullo! That Bychester? Who is that speaking? . . . *Who?* . . . Oh, Mariella! I didn't recognize your voice. Thought you were Jessie.' (Jessie was the Monkhouses' kitchen-maid.) '. . . You've come over for Jas? Good! Shan't mind seeing the last of *her*, I can tell you! Let me down pretty badly did that mare yesterday. Haven't got over it yet! I thought she was a better nag. . . What's that you say? Oh, where am I speaking from? Well, I'm over at Dewburn – yes, Dewburn Hall, the Eliots' place, you know. Met them in Hordon, and they asked me over here. Patience is home, you know, from her Paris school, and guess what – she's going up to Sadler's Wells – yes, the ballet school – for her last year. . . Yes, I thought you'd be surprised. She's been learning ballet in Paris, and she's got frightfully keen. How she managed to persuade her father to let her go on with it, goodness knows! Nobody's more surprised than Patience! Sticky old bird is old Eliot! Perhaps it was because Lady Bailey (you know the Baileys of Twyford – well, she's one of the sisters) offered to put Patience up in her London house. Ursula Bailey is a great friend of old Eliot. Patience thinks it must be that, anyway. . . Honestly, Mariella, you wouldn't know Patience now. She's quite grown p, though she's only sixteen, and she's devastatingly pretty. She's got – what shall I call it? *Chic*, I suppose you'd say, and no wonder, seeing that she's half French. And then, of course, a year or so at a Paris finishing school does that for you! . . . Now look, Mariella, will you tell the mater I shan't be home for dinner – I'm having it here – but I shall be over straight afterwards – eight o'clockish – to get into my evening clothes. I'm taking Patience to the Hunt Ball in Newcastle. She's going back to school tomorrow, so it's up to me to give the kid a good time. Of course, she's far too young, really, but she *looks* seventeen at least. We rang up old Eliot and asked permission, and he said it was OK as long as she was with *me*. Tell the mater I shall want the big car – less draughty for Patience than the sports, and you know ballet dancers can't be too careful. . . By the way, when do you go back, Mariella? Yes, I mean to the daily grind? Oh, tonight! Shame! Oh, well – every holiday has to come to an end, hasn't it, and you managed the Horse Sports anyway. My love to Edinburgh! 'Bye!'

Mariella laid down the receiver. She had hardly said a word! It had been one long eulogy on Patience Eliot! Patience was pretty; Patience had *chic*; Patience was going to the Hunt Ball in her, Mariella's, place. A girl with a less generous nature than Mariella would have hated Patience at that moment. But Mariella merely sighed and thought: 'Lucky, lucky Patience to be going to the Hunt Ball with Nigel!'

Chapter 2

Himself of Inveross

Mariella left Bychester as soon as she could after tea, and rode away on Jasmine Flower, with Lady Jane on a leading-rein, in the direction of Hordon Castle, the Charltons' home. As she neared the old border fortress, she saw a lone horseman approaching, and in a moment or two, she recognized Guy himself.

'Oh, hullo, Mariella!' he said. 'You know, you ought to have let me come over for that mare.'

'Oh, it's quite all right, Guy,' Mariella assured him. 'I had to come over to Bychester in any case to collect Jasmine Flower. What's happened, Guy? Have you come into a fortune? You look on top of the world!'

'I *am* on top of the world!' laughed Guy – Mariella had never seen him like this before. 'Congratulate me, Mariella – I'm going to be married!'

'M-married?' gasped Mariella. 'But who to? You mean – you can't mean—'

'Yes, I can!' said Guy. 'I mean Jane!' He wheeled his horse and rode along beside her.

'Jane? But I thought – you told me – I mean I always understood—'

'That Jane was wedded to her art? Well, she's a woman and she's changed her mind. Women sometimes do, you know!'

'I didn't think Jane would,' said Mariella bluntly. 'Of course, I knew some time ago that she was most awfully fond of you, Guy. Still—'

'Well, there it is,' said Guy. 'She sent me a wire yesterday. It came after I got home. She must have sent it just after the Gala performance, and it said she'd decided to leave the Wells. Like you, I could scarcely believe it, so I rang her up to make sure, and it's true. She feels she has got to the top of her profession, and she means to stop while she is still there. I dare say caring for me had something to do with it, too.'

'Of course it had. It had *everything* to do with it!' cried Mariella. 'Guy, you *are* a modest person! Well, when is Jane coming home, and when is the wedding to be?'

'Oh, not for some time yet, I'm afraid,' answered Guy. 'The telegram saying: "I've left the Wells" was just Jane's dramatic way of saying she had changed her mind and was going to marry me. Of course she can't walk out – just like that! There is her contract, for one thing. Anyway, she woud never leave them in the middle of the season – especially when so many of their dancers are *hors de combat* – Yvonne Chévier in Milan, and Wendy Wesley in Australia, and somebody else in hospital with appendicitis – not to mention Veronica Weston having a baby! If Jane were in the mere *corps de ballet* it might be different, but as it is, it will be months before she can actually leave the Wells. She explained that on the phone. We aren't announcing our engagement for a bit, as a matter of fact.'

'Oh, Guy – why not?' demanded Mariella. 'Or shouldn't I ask?'

Guy laughed.

'It's just that Jane wants me to do something before we're actually engaged,' he explained. 'It's a sort of joke between us, and yet deadly serious, if you see what I mean.'

'No, I don't,' said Mariella. 'But I'll take your word for it, and I hope you'll be very, very happy, Guy. I'm sure you will be – you're both such darlings!' She gave a little sigh. She wasn't feeling very happy, herself, just at the moment.

'Well, here we are,' Guy said, as they reached the gateway leading into the courtyard of the old castle. 'Come in and have some tea, Mariella.' Though he said nothing, he had heard the sigh and guessed the reason for it.

'Thanks, Guy, but I've just had some,' said Mariella, dismounting and leading Lady Jane into the loose-box Guy indicated. 'I had it with Lady Monkhouse.' She couldn't help making a naughty face. 'Aunt Phyllis has lost her kennel-maid – the third since Harriet Dickson!'

'So she made use of you, eh?' said Guy, looking so stern that Mariella interposed nervously:

'Oh, no, Guy, you're wrong. I *offered* to do it – I mean to muck out the stables. I wanted to help Aunt Phyllis.'

'And what about Nigel? Was he helping, too?' demanded Guy.

'Oh, no, Nigel wasn't there. I did hope he'd get back in time for tea, but he rang up to say he was having a meal with the Eliots of Dewburn. Matter of fact,' Mariella tried to sound very casual and offhanded, 'he's taking Patience to the Hunt Ball in Newcastle tonight.'

Guy wasn't deceived. He looked down at her face and saw the misery in her blue eyes. He was filled with fury to think of Nigel Monkhouse daring to make her unhappy. He was very fond of Mariella.

It was just at this moment that a tall figure came into the courtyard from the other side – the side where the surgery was. He was an immensely tall fair young man with a rugged face and deep-set blue eyes.

'Like an eagle,' thought Mariella instantly. 'But I'm sure I've seen him somewhere before. Now where can I have met him?'

'Oh, hullo, Robin,' said Guy. 'You remember Robin, Mariella? He is a veterinary surgeon, too, and has come to give me a hand.'

58

'I'm sorry,' apologized Mariella. 'I know your face quite well, but I can't think where we met.'

The young man leaned down towards her (he had to do so to reach her) and shook hands very ceremoniously.

'Robin Campbell,' he said in a slow, deep voice. 'We met at Inveross at Hogmanay.'

'Oh, *now* I remember!' exclaimed Mariella. 'You are "Himself of Inveross!" No wonder I didn't recognize you. You were wearing a wonderful costume on that night – a kilt and all the trimmings!'

'We were just talking about the Hunt Ball that is being held in Newcastle this evening,' said Guy. 'You were saying you wanted to go, Robin – if you could find a partner. I was about to persuade Mariella . . .' His steady grey eyes met Robin Campbell's blue ones over the top of Mariella's red-gold head. 'Don't give me away, old chap,' said the glance. 'Ask the kid to go with you.'

Robin Campbell rose to the occasion with true Highland chivalry.

'I am hoping you have succeeded,' he said. 'There is nothing that I should like to do more than to go to the Hunt Ball this evening – if I could find a partner. Would you come to my rescue, Miss Foster?'

'Call me Mariella, please,' said the girl. 'I'd adore to go with you.' Her heart felt a little less sore. At all events, she wasn't going to miss the ball altogether, even if she hadn't the partner she would have chosen. Also – there was no getting away from it – this young man was nice. He wouldn't be Guy's friend if he wasn't, thought Mariella. Dear Guy! Lucky, lucky Jane to have fallen in love with Guy, and he with her!

'There's only one thing,' added Mariella to the young man, 'I shan't be able to stay until the end of the dance. I have my train to Edinburgh to catch. It's somewhere about midnight.'

'That is quite all right,' said Robin in his precise, Highland voice. 'Until midnight it shall be. Then you will disappear – just like Cinderella!'

So it happened that Nigel, dancing a waltz with Patience, beheld Mariella in a ball-gown of sea-green tulle enter the ballroom on the arm of an immensely tall young man in full Highland evening dress. The two of them made such a striking picture that heads turned to look at them, and people asked each other who they were.

'Good Lord!' burst out Nigel. 'Look at the fellow Mariella's got in tow! Wonder where she picked him up?'

'Oh, I think he's *wonderful!*' said Patience. 'Not handsome, of course, but something much more dramatic. Splendid, I think you'd call it!'

'U-um,' said Nigel grudgingly. 'A bit *over* dramatic, if you ask me! Fellow's making a spectacle of himself!'

'Of course he is!' exclaimed Patience. 'All Highlanders make spectacles of themselves. They adore showing off, and why shouldn't they? When they've got such a wonderful national costume – why shouldn't they show it off?' It isn't as if they aren't as brave as brave. Why, look at the Highland regiments! They go into battle swinging their kilts and scaring the enemy to death, and fighting to the last man! I think they're perfectly wonderful!'

Nigel stared down at her, displeased. She was pretty, certainly, but very, very young. Most undiplomatic, and yes – you might almost call it *gauche*. He began to feel it had been a mistake on his part to bring her to the ball. She's done nothing but talk about the charm of Highlanders so far! He almost wished he'd brought Mariella instead!

Mariella, to her surprise, found that although she wasn't dancing with Nigel, she was still having a lovely time. In fact, the time of her life! Robin, like most Scotsmen, was a born dancer, and carried his six feet two inches lightly.

Never had Mariella enjoyed an Eightsome Reel so much! There were several members of the Scottish Folk Dance Society present, and they very soon collected round Himself of Inveross whom most of them seemed to know by sight, and the rest of the ballroom cast envious glances at the set of whirling, yelling Highlanders. Mariella was almost danced off her feet! There was no time for her even to *think* of Nigel!

Chapter 3

Phone Call from Northumberland

After the mid-term break, time went by quickly for Mariella. Easter came and went, and the summer term began. Working away in her rooms up in Edinburgh, she suddenly realized that in a few weeks' time she would be home again for the long vacation. But before that, came her exam (Mariella shivered at the thought of it – her first exam in her career as veterinary surgeon). Then, after that, came various end-of-term frivolities – an inter-collegiate dance, an inter-varsity debate, and several concerts. Besides all these, she'd just had a letter from Jane to say that the Sadler's Wells Theatre Ballet was visiting Edinburgh just a week before vacation began, and that Jane was coming with them as guest artist.

'Dear Mariella,' wrote Jane, 'now that the furore has died down – about my leaving the Wells, I mean – I can write to you in a calm frame of mind! Of course everyone here thinks I'm quite mad, but I know I'm not. I've had my triumphs – enough to last me the rest of my life! I have far too much North Country blood in me to be able to live in a city all my life. Why, even now, I'm longing for the sight and sound of the country! Not that I'm like *you*, of course, Mariella – thinking of nothing but riding, and stables, and looking after sick animals (though I must admit I loved riding Lady Jane), but I keep thinking of the daffodils fringing the lawns at Monks Hollow, and the moors all misty and pearl-coloured in the spring sunshine. Oh, well – next year I shall be there to see them!

'I am really writing to tell you that I shall be coming up to Edinburgh to dance as guest artist with the Theatre Ballet at the end of this month. I am dancing the leading role here at Covent Garden in *Coppélia* on the Friday night, and I thought of catching the night train – I could just do it – and going straight to Loch Awe, meeting Guy there, and having one glorious day climbing Ben Cruachan, then dashing back to Edinburgh on the Sunday night. Oh, I know it sounds idiotic, when it was Ben Cruachan that nearly finished me off at Christmas, but the weather's lovely now, and I'm sure I'll be quite safe with Guy.

'And by the way, I went to Harrods yesterday and got all the right things to climb in – a wind-jacket like they wear on Mount Everest expeditions, trousers, and wonderful climbing boots. I got some neatsfoot oil to put on them. That's to make them soft, Guy says, so that they don't skin your ankles. It makes them waterproof, too. Not that anything's *really* waterproof in Scotland, Guy says!

'It will be a month or two yet before my contract runs out and I'm able really to leave the Wells. When I do, I expect we shall be getting married straight away. And while I think of it – will you be my chief bridesmaid, Mariella?'

'Of course I will,' said Mariella aloud. 'I wonder who the best man will be? Not Nigel certainly! Jane and he don't get on together, and I don't think that Guy approves of Nigel, either. I expect it will be Robin Campbell – Himself of Inveross. Robin seems to be Guy's best friend.'

She turned to the letter again.

'Isn't it strange,' wrote Jane, 'how people gravitate to the Wells! Guess who the latest is? Patience Eliot, David's little half-sister! Of course, she isn't so little now – she's sixteen – and she's partly French, so dancing's probably in her blood! Anyway, she's staying with Lady Bailey – you remember, the person I threw my ballet shoes at the awful day when I was unmasked! She – I mean Patience – came

63

to my dressing-room the other night, and we had a long talk all about Northumberland. It made me quite homesick!

'I've seen a lot of Veronica lately. She came to my dressing-room on the Gala night, just before the performance, to wish me luck. A reporter sneaked in, and of course it was all in the papers! I expect you saw it. She didn't stay for the performance. That would have been too nerve-racking for me, and too harrowing for her – seeing someone else dancing her role in a Gala. She is coming home soon to Bracken, and will stay there until her baby is born. Sebastian will fly up at weekends whenever possible. Veronica has promised to present the certificates and prizes at Miss Martin's Charity Matinée shortly. It's for the RSPCA, and of course it will make all the difference to have Veronica there. People will go in droves just to *see* her – even if she isn't dancing! Veronica says Miss Martin helped her so much at the beginning of her career that she feels she owes her a terrific debt, so if she can help her in any way, she does. And, by the way, Veronica was to have appeared in the television programme of *Swan Lake*, but of course she can't, so they are going to use a film. Sebastian is conducting.

'I really must stop writing now, and go to bed. It's very late, and I have a hard day tomorrow. I never seem to have time to do anything for myself – like writing letters – until after midnight!

'Lots of love as ever,
'Jane.

'PS – I went to the New Theatre to see Rosita and Angelo the other night. They're terrific! It's the only word! Everyone is raving about them. Angelo's *zapateado* is unbelievable, and Rosita is so beautiful and full of fire. They have the most amazing wardrobe, and how they manage to change costumes so quickly is nothing short of a miracle!

They must have a host of dressers behind the scenes to help them!

'Uncle Oscar went with me, and he wrote a crit in the *Ballet Weekly* – all about two of the most talented and promising young Spanish dancers London has seen for a very long time. I think he's ever so proud to feel that Caroline (I should say Rosita!) lived in his home, and began her career as a Spanish dancer from under his very roof, so to speak, though he confessed he was puzzled by her at that time. He knew she hadn't the technique ever to make a classical ballet dancer. Even he (wise old bird as your father is, Mariella!) never thought of Spanish dancing. And now she and Angelo are among the World's Great Ones!

'Well, this really *is* the end of my letter. Good-bye again!

'Jane.'

Mariella laid down the letter, and for a moment her thoughts flew back to her own home in London, 140(a) Fortnum Mansions. She thought of her mother, dark-eyed and slender, gliding gracefully in and out between ballet performances when she, Mariella, was a small girl. Later on, her beautiful mother disappearing for long months when, in an advisory capacity, she toured with one or other of the companies, leaving behind her a small, lonely girl – the child who was Mariella in those far-off days. While she sat there, Jane's letter on her knee, Mariella lived again the long, lonely days. They were busy days, too, filled with detested ballet classes in Madame Viret's school, days when Maestro (Ivan Stcherbakof), Madame's friend and assistant, had shouted at her, scolded her, despised her. The never-to-be-forgotten afternoon when she and Jane had sat by the lake in Regent's Park and fed the ducks, and had decided to change places – Jane to go to the audition at Sadler's Wells in Mariella's place. Mad, mad plot that had succeeded in a quite dramatic way!

Suddenly her thoughts were rudely interrupted by the ringing of the telephone in the lobby outside, and Mariella rushed to answer it.

'A Mr Monkhouse is calling you (personally) from Newcastle,' said the voice of the telephone operator, 'and wishes to know whether you are willing to pay for the call?'

'Oh – er – yes, of course,' answered Mariella. 'Hullo, Nigel!'

'Hullo!' said Nigel's voice, sounding thin and reedy because of the distance, and not a bit like his usual aggressive tones. 'That Mariella? Good! Sorry I had no loose change on me, but I knew you wouldn't mind a "reverse". Fact is, Mariella, one or two of us over here thought we'd like to come up for the end-of-term jollities – the ballet and what not. How about it?'

Mariella's head swam with delight.

'Oh, that would be *lovely!*' she said.

'Yes, I thought the idea might appeal to you,' went on Nigel. 'There will be five of us at this end – myself, Robin Campbell (oh yes, he wants to come, he says. Goodness knows why! But as a matter of fact he'll be quite useful. We can come in his car – it's huge), Fiona and Ian. Oh, and of course, Guy Charlton. He wants to see Jane dance, or something. So there will be six altogether – counting you. Can you get the tickets – for the ballet, I mean? Easier at your end. Don't leave it too late, old girl, will you, or they'll be sold out. Oh, and there's the question of digs. Charlton wants to stay at the Trossachs, because Jane will be staying there with the company, but it's a bit steep for Campbell and me. So how about your place? Think they'd put us up? . . . Right-ho, then! Oh, Fiona and Ian? They're staying at the Waverley. That comes of being near-millionaires! . . . Well, see what you can do, there's a good girl, and give me a tinkle. I might think of something else we'd like to go to in the meantime. . . Well, how are things going up at your end? They're fine here. Mother's got a new filly, Red Pepper. She's out of Challenger – you know, Mrs Woodruff's wonderful mare – by Gold Cross, so she ought to be a winner! . . .'

'Oh, there go the pips, Nigel,' Mariella said regretfully. 'Good-bye! What's that? . . .'

'I was telling you about Red Pepper,' went on Nigel. 'She's—'

'But Nigel, hadn't we better—'

It was no use. Nigel was off on his favourite hobby-horse, and nothing – certainly not the mere warning pips of a long-distance telephone call – would stop him, especially if somebody else was paying for the call! The minutes went by, and two more lots of pips sounded in Mariella's anxious ears before he eventually rang off with a final: 'Don't forget those tickets – six of them. 'Bye.'

'Good-bye, Nigel,' said Mariella, putting down the receiver with a sigh. Nine minutes! It was going to be an expensive call. But then, Nigel always ignored telephone calls. All her other boy-friends (and girl-friends, too, for the matter of that) left the money discreetly beside the telephone when they used it. But not Nigel! He just used it in a lordly manner, and thanked you very charmingly afterwards – charm was Nigel's strong suit! Also, he was always 'out of small change' when there was a trunk call to make! Yes, Mariella knew in her heart of hearts that Nigel was extremely slack about money matters, that he was more than a bit of a scrounger – though she wouldn't have admitted it, even to herself. Not once, but many times, had he asked her to get tickets for the two of them for a concert or theatre, and never remembered to repay her. Once she'd even bought a large and expensive bottle of liniment for his horse out of her own money, and when at last, driven by sheer bankruptcy, she had asked him for the money, he had flown at her.

67

'Why on earth didn't you *ask* me for it, Mariella?'

'I didn't like to,' she faltered. 'A girl doesn't like asking a man for money.'

'Why not, in the name of goodness!' exclaimed Nigel. 'How much is it, anyway?'

'Quite a lot,' said Mariella, turning pink. 'You see, there were the tickets for that concert we went to at the City Hall last December, and the Cricket Club Dance at Bychester, and the liniment for Pollix—'

'Oh, *no!*' broke in Nigel. 'You *can't* say I didn't pay you for that! Why, it's *months* ago. I swear I paid you for it. I remember distinctly.'

'No, you didn't, Nigel – really you didn't.'

'Oh, well – if you say so, I suppose I can't have. But I must say it seems very odd and not a bit like me. I'm so particular. Another time, Mariella, please ask me at once. I don't like things going on mounting up. I can't keep track of them.'

'I *did* ask you, Nigel,' said poor Mariella. 'Only you still didn't give it to me.'

'Well, why didn't you remind me,' said Nigel. 'Good Lord! What a fuss about money! I had no idea you were so mercenary.'

Mariella's blue eyes filled with tears.

'One's got to think about money when one's only got an allowance,' she told him. 'You see, Nigel, I haven't got a job yet, like you. I just have what Mummy gives me, and it isn't all that much. It costs a lot to live here at college.'

'All right! All right! Don't nag!' said Nigel. 'Here's ten quid. You can hang on to the change, if you're all that hard up.'

Mariella had taken the note he held out and put it into her empty notecase. She didn't dare to say that the amount Nigel owed her was more – much more – than that. She was thankful for small mercies! She vowed that she would never pay for Nigel's tickets unless he actually gave her the money first. And now here she was doing it again! But what else could she do? She couldn't very well ask him to send her a cheque before she got them. If she did that, the tickets would probably all be gone. No, she'd have to risk it just once more, and be firm with Nigel. Very firm!

Chapter 4

Mariella Has Visitors

Mariella was all excitement when the day drew near for her friends to arrive. She was looking her best in a pale blue sweater and skirt. Her eyes sparkled, and her auburn hair shone with youth and health. She was feeling on top of the world! Her exam was over, and she'd just heard this morning that she'd passed. Besides all this, at any moment now she'd hear a car draw up outside Craigmuir, which was the name of the house where she stayed, and she'd see Nigel getting out – Nigel with his fair, shining head and broad shoulders. Of course, Guy and Robin would be there, too, so she wouldn't have Nigel all to herself. Still, it would be nice to see Guy and Robin as well.

She had arranged the tea trolley herself, and it was laden with good things – all the nicest cakes and the juiciest sausage-rolls the Edinburgh shops could provide. She had bought them with her own money, and spent almost her last penny to do so. After all, you couldn't expect a mere landlady to think of the sausage-rolls and éclairs that Nigel loved, could you? She had just shaken up the cushions on the settee for the fifth time, when she heard the sound of a car drawing up outside the house. They'd arrived!

She dashed to the window and looked down. Yes, there they were – three young men just getting out of the car. Guy, tall and dark, hauling out the cases; Nigel, his fair, curly hair glinting in the sunlight, directing operations; Robin Campbell, taller than any of them, looking up at the window and waving to her.

'He's so nice!' thought Mariella, waving back. 'If it wasn't for Nigel. . .'

Then Nigel saw her, too, and smiled, and Mariella's heart fluttered. He was so handsome! So masterful! You couldn't help loving him! He took the steps in a couple of strides, followed by the others, and in another minute they were all in the hall laughing and chattering like a lot of magpies.

'Splendid run . . . Cheviots wonderful, and all the Border country looking beautiful . . . did seventy most of the way . . . average of fifty over the run . . . got a glimpse of Holy Island, yes, Lindisfarne . . . Fiona and Ian coming on behind in Fiona's little sports car . . . staying at the Waverley, but of course you know . . . How did the exam go, Mariella?' (This in Robin's soft Highland voice.) '. . . Splendid news! May I offer you my sincere congratulations! . . . Oh, so you've passed? Wonders will never cease!' (This Nigel.) 'You must have more brains than I thought. Congratters, old girl!'

They soon made short work of the plates of cakes and sausage-rolls, and also a mountain of hot buttered scones put before them by Mrs McDougal, who thought she had never seen three more splendid young men. She liked Guy because he opened the door for her, and Robin because he took the tray out of her hands with grave courtesy, and because he was Highland Scots. Och, yes – it was pairfectly plain by his voice! Nigel charmed her, too, though he didn't actually do anything for her, but he gave her a wink with one blue eye that made her his slave. Nigel was always very careful to keep in with landladies, as he afterwards told Mariella.

'Did you manage the tickets all right?' he asked, as they lingered over third and fourth cups of tea. 'Cigarette, Charlton? . . . Oh, of course, stupid of me. I forgot you don't smoke. . . Campbell?'

'I am after smoking my old pipe, thank you,' said the

71

Scotsman. 'I am liking it better!'

'Oh, yes, I got the tickets,' said Mariella, after she had supplied Robin with matches and Nigel with an ashtray. 'Six in the Upper Circle.'

'Upper Circle?' repeated Nigel. 'For the love of mike, why the Upper Circle? Weren't there any in the Stalls or Grand Circle?'

Mariella turned pink. How was she to explain that she just hadn't had the spare cash for six seats in the Grand Circle. As it was, she hoped Nigel would remember to pay her back before he went home; otherwise she'd be sunk! There were such a lot of odd things to pay for at the end of the summer term. She decided to tell a white lie – a very white one, since there was a good deal of truth in it.

'As a matter of fact, the Upper Circle is the best place in the theatre to see the ballet from,' she told him. 'Didn't you know?'

Nigel was rather taken aback.

'Can't say I did,' he declared.

'Oh, yes – I have heard that that is so,' said Robin. 'In any case, I am quite sure that Mariella's choice of seats for us will be admirable. It was indeed good of you to go to all the trouble of getting them for us, Mariella. We are very grateful.'

'Hear! Hear!' put in Guy, pouring himself out a fifth cup of tea. 'By the way, I'm off straight away, Mariella – to the station I mean. I want to be in Dalmally late tonight.'

'Dalmally? Aren't you going to Inveross, Robin's home?' exclaimed Mariella in surprise. 'I was sure you'd go there.'

'Not tonight,' said Guy. 'Jane will be at the Allt Nan Ros and I don't wish to meet her at the hotel, but on the slopes of Beinn a' Bhùiridh.'

'On the slopes of – of that unpronounceable mountain! What ever for?' said Mariella.

'That is a secret between myself and Jane!' laughed Guy.

'Robin is coming over by car tomorrow,' he went on. 'Just to say how d'you do to his people. He and Jane and I are going to have dinner together – to celebrate Jane's and my ascent of Ben Cruachan!' He thought: 'Yes, and our engagement, too, for I mean to ask Jane to marry me formally on the top of Ben Cruachan!' But he kept his thoughts to himself. They were too sacred to be shared even with his friends. 'You know, Robin hasn't properly met Jane yet – unless you could count that time he rowed her across the loch, and she called him "my man"!'

'Did she really!' exclaimed Nigel. 'I hadn't heard that one! I must say, it's just like Jane. She always was loopy!'

'On the contrary, she was very charming,' said Robin Campbell stiffly. Mariella got the impression that there wasn't much love lost between Nigel and Himself of Inveross.

'Look, Mariella,' put in Guy, seeing that the atmosphere was becoming chilly, 'your exam is over, and the ballet isn't till Monday, so what about coming over to Inveross with Robin tomorrow? It would be a nice drive for you, and company for Robin.'

Robin Campbell leaned down towards Mariella, and said: 'It would indeed be a pleasure if you would do so.'

'Hey? Hold on a bit!' put in Nigel. 'What about *me?* Mariella's going to climb Arthur's Seat with me, aren't you, Mariella?'

This was the first Mariella had heard of it, but Nigel made it sound as if it were a date of long standing. Anyway, she was only too willing to climb Arthur's Seat, Nelson's Column, the Eiffel Tower, or indeed anything else with Nigel at her side!

'Oh, yes – that would be *lovely!*' she said. 'I'm so sorry, Robin. If it hadn't been for – well, you see how it is.'

'Yes, I am seeing how it is,' answered Robin gravely.

The three of them had a splendid dinner at the Waverley

Hotel with Ian and Fiona. Fiona wore a black lace evening dress with black lace slippers to match, and with her fair hair and skin she looked a picture. Nevertheless, she didn't seem very pleased with life.

'It's a most awful bore,' she complained to Mariella, 'we've got to go and have dinner tomorrow night with Ian's ghastly uncle. *Why*, I can't think! He's the most dreadful old man, with one hand that shakes all the time. He makes me feel quite sick!'

'Uncle William is ninety-four, and he may pop off at any minute,' said Ian, lighting a cigarette.

'Well, what if he does?' demanded Fiona, shrugging her white shoulders. 'He can pop off for all I care! If you ask me, he's been here too long. No one ought to be allowed to live till they're ninety-four!'

'I quite agree,' said Ian. 'But things being as they are, it's just as well if we keep on reminding uncle that we're here and that we're his relatives. These old fogies get absent-minded, and he might forget about us in his will!'

'Oh, *money!*' ejaculated Fiona.

'It's all very well for you to say, "Oh, *money*" like that,' said Ian. 'It isn't *you* who goes short if there isn't enough to go round. *Your* latest fur coat has to be paid for, even if *I* have to go on running the same old car year after year.'

'It's only two years old,' said Fiona. 'Mine's the same.'

'You only use yours for shopping. It ought to last for ever.'

'Well, it isn't going to, my dear. I've ordered a new one, and it'll be here any day now.'

'There you are!' exclaimed Ian in exasperation. 'What did I say? It's a good thing *someone* in this family has got a little horse-sense. We go to see Uncle William tomorrow, and you'll try to be charming to him, Fiona.'

'Oh, all right,' agreed Fiona. 'How I wish it was over! But I suppose you're right for once, Ian, and we must try to

74

please the old boy. You don't know you're lucky, Mariella, not to be married, and have all these things to worry about.'

Mariella laughed ruefully. Her anxieties were just as heavy – if somewhat more mundane – than worrying about how to pay for a new sports car. She was wondering how to make her allowance last till the end of the term, just supposing Nigel – oh, well, it was no use spoiling the evening. She must just wait and hope!

'How is Flora?' she asked Fiona.

Fiona dismissed her daughter with a shrug.

'Oh, *she's* all right. Nothing ever happens to Flora. I think I'm really a model mother! I never *fuss* over the child, like some mothers fuss over their disgusting babies. I never talk "baby talk" to her. I never pamper her.'

'In short, you don't know she's there at all,' thought Mariella, who had heard about Fiona's treatment of the infant Flora. 'You might as well not have a baby at all!' Aloud she said: 'I suppose you left her with your mother?'

'Oh, no,' answered Fiona. 'Mummy's in London, so I wasn't able to do that. I tried all my friends, and would you believe it, not one of them was the least use. So in the end I just had to leave Flora at home and bribe Ruby to stay and look after her. *Bribe* is the word! I had to give the girl a really *fabulous* sum – nearly as much as my permanent wave! These girls won't do *anything* unless you pay them the earth!' She sounded like a younger edition of Aunt Phyllis, thought Mariella.

At eleven o'clock Nigel, Robin, and she went home to Craigmuir, and after a cup of coffee they went to bed.

Next morning they were up early. It was a lovely day and, out of the window, away beyond the houses, Mariella could catch a glimpse of Edinburgh Castle, and the Old Town climbing up to it like a wicked snake. Robin Campbell came and stood behind her.

'Not that it's wicked now, but it used to be,' she said aloud.

'You are meaning the Old Town. Yes, it is now less picturesque, but also less full of vice,' said Robin. 'Ah, I see one just catches a glimpse of Arthur's Seat over the roof-tops there. It is a perfect day for a climb. You will enjoy it.'

'Yes, I'm looking forward to it so much,' admitted Mariella. 'Of course I might have gone up there many times by myself if I had wished, but it's not the same. You need someone to share it with.'

'That is true,' agreed Robin.

'What's true?' demanded Nigel, coming up behind them, and putting his hands possessively on Mariella's shoulders.

'We were saying that climbing Arthur's Seat by oneself is not the same as doing it with a companion,' answered Robin. 'Especially with such a charming companion.' He looked at Mariella with open admiration.

'You'll make the girl swollen-headed,' said Nigel, but he was quite pleased. He liked Mariella to be admired, as long as she made it quite clear that she preferred him. 'But you're right, Robin – Mariella's no end of a sport. *She* wouldn't go making a chap carry all her stuff, holding him up. She's as good as a man, aren't you, Mariella, old girl?'

'Oh, surely, Monkhouse – you don't want Mariella to be like a man?' expostulated Robin. 'In any case, it is quite impossible. Mariella is the most feminine of girls.'

'Oh, yes of course – but you know what I mean. She doesn't want you to be looking after her every moment of the time.'

'It wouldn't matter if I did want him to,' thought Mariella, a little wistfully. 'Nigel wouldn't do it. Nigel never *thinks* of looking after me. He's too *used* to me!'

'Well, I'm afraid I must be off,' said Robin, taking a last look at the misty blue hump that was Arthur's Seat. 'I have a little business to do in town before I go. So long, both of you! I shall see you tomorrow evening when I get back.'

'Good-bye, Robin,' said Mariella. Out of the window she watched him stride off down the street towards the garage where he had left his car, and she sighed, though she didn't know why. It was as if she had a lost a very dear friend. But that was ridiculous – he had only gone for a day. He would be back again tomorrow evening, as he said. Her thoughts were interrupted by the sound of the telephone, and a moment or two later Mrs McDougal put her head round the door.

'It's a call for you, Mr Monkhouse,' she said. 'A gentleman speaking frae the riding-school awa doon by Holyrood. His name is Mistair O'Dowd, I ondairstand him to say.'

'Jock O'Dowd, by jove!' exclaimed Nigel. 'Good old Jock! I wonder how he knows I'm here?' He dashed out of the room, and a moment later Mariella heard him greeting the unknown Jock like a long-lost friend. . . 'That you, Jock? Monkhouse here! . . . Yes, of course . . . of course, old chap . . . sounds just the thing. . . What's that? This afternoon? Look, Jock, old chap, it's a bit awkward. You see . . . oh well, if it's like that, it can't be helped. . . Oh, she'll understand. As you say, it's the only possible . . . right-ho! See you two-ish. 'Bye!'

Mariella, standing by the window – was filled with fore-boding. Her day on the mountain – her bright and glorious day with Nigel – was going to be snatched from her after all. She knew it! Snatched from her by one Jock O'Dowd! When Nigel came back into the room, casually lighting a cigarette, she knew before he spoke what he was going to say.

'Look, Mariella – I'm most frightfully sorry, old girl, but I just can't make Arthur's Seat today. No, you see that fellow that just rang up – Jock O'Dowd – has a mare he wants me to see. Just the thing for the mater. Oh, I know she's got the filly, but she's only rising three. Bit young for the mater. Charlton's mare would have been just the ticket, but you know Charlton. Obstinate as they make 'em! Wouldn't sell. Offered him the earth. Fellow's got too much money if you ask me! Well, O'Dowd says he's got a mare that'll make rings round Lady Jane, and *he* ought to know. Jock sold that mare to Charlton. Trouble is that Jock is going to Dumfries tonight, so the only time he can put the mare through her paces for me is this afternoon.'

'Couldn't someone else—' began Mariella, a sick feeling at her heart.

'There just *is* no one else, said Nigel. 'At least, nobody like Jock. Besides, dash it all, I want to see Jock. He's a great friend of mine and I haven't seen him in years. You surely wouldn't want me to miss an opportunity like this, Mariella? Anyway, Arthur's Seat is a bit of a sweat, isn't it? Hours of slogging, and then, when you get to the top, what do you see?'

'I don't know,' said Mariella. 'I've never been there.'

'Neither have I, come to that,' admitted Nigel, 'but I can imagine it well enough! It'll be blessed cold, I shouldn't wonder – probably a mist. And all around, nothing but hills and things. Confoundedly depressing, if you ask me! I'm dashed if I know why you ever suggested it. Tell you what – why don't you come down to the riding-school with me, Mariella, and see old Jock? You could give me the benefit of your opinion. I value your opinion on horseflesh very highly, you know, Mariella. I always say: "Mariella knows more about horseflesh than any woman I know, except perhaps the mater." Well, what do you say?'

A few days ago Mariella would have said: 'Very well, Nigel,' as meek as a mouse. But for some reason, she wasn't feeling quite so meek this morning.

'No, thank you, Nigel,' she said. 'I don't think I'll come

down there. I'll do some shopping instead.'

'Right-ho,' agreed Nigel. 'Just as you like, of course, but don't say I haven't asked you.'

'I won't,' said Mariella.

She ran into the kitchen to tell Mrs McDougal that they wouldn't be needing any sandwiches, and that she would be in for lunch after all.

'And the young gentleman?' asked Mrs McDougal.

'Oh, he's having lunch down at the riding-school – the McCreedy Livery Stables, I think he said it was called,' Mariella said, with a little sigh. 'So I'll be all on my own, Mrs McDougal.'

'Puir wee lamb!' thought the kind Scotswoman. 'Head o'er heels in love with that young man she is, and him not knowing nor caring the snap o' his fingers for her, and her as pretty as a picture!' Her views on Nigel's charms had altered a bit since last night. Like most Scotswomen she was astute. As Nigel himself would have said – there were no flies on Margaret McDougal!

'Och, he's no guid enough for her,' she added mentally. 'For masel', I prefair the other tall young man. He has the kinder face!'

Chapter 5

Arthur's Seat

Mariella walked slowly up Princes Street looking in all the shop windows. She hadn't any money to buy anything, but that didn't matter because her thoughts were elsewhere, and she didn't see the goods displayed. She was thinking about Arthur's Seat and how lovely it would have been walking up to the top with Nigel. She was so deep in her thoughts that she nearly had a head-on collision with someone coming in the opposite direction.

'Oh, I'm *so* sorry!' she gasped. Then, looking up, she found herself gazing straight into the blue eyes of Himself of Inveross.

'But I thought . . .' they began both together. Then Robin recovered from his surprise. 'I am thinking that you were far away up on yon mountain?' He nodded over his shoulder at the ever present summit of Arthur's Seat peeping over the top of the station.

'It's all off!' said Mariella with a laugh. She mustn't show him how disappointed she was. She had her pride. 'Nigel got a phone call, and he had to go and meet a friend.' Then suddenly she felt that here was someone with whom she needn't keep up appearances. Robin wouldn't think any the less of her because Nigel treated her lightly. Robin would understand.

'Oh, Robin,' she said, 'I'm feeling so miserable! It's such a lovely, lovely day, and here I am. . .' She motioned towards the shops outside which were collecting the usual crowd of shop-gazers, although it was yet quite early in the morning. 'To think that I might be up there on that lovely, blue mountain! Oh, well – I suppose it can't be helped. But how are *you* here? I thought you would be halfway to Loch Awe by now!'

'I had a little business to do before I set off,' he answered. 'But now we have fortunately met, can I not persuade you to change your mind and come with me, Mariella?'

Mariella hesitated. For a moment she was tempted – sorely tempted – to accept his offer. It would serve Nigel right if he came home and found that the bird had flown. Then she remembered that it was Sunday tomorrow, and she'd planned to go to St Giles with Nigel. She'd hate to miss that.

'Oh, no, thank you, Robin,' she said, 'I couldn't do that. Nigel would never forgive me.'

'Well, I shall tell you what it is we are doing,' said the young man. 'I am taking you up to Arthur's Seat, myself.'

'Oh, but Robin—'

'Now do not argue. My mind is quite made up.'

'But your hotel at Inveross?'

'Och, my hotel! It will get along perfectly well without me for a wee while longer. I can come up again before long.'

'But Jane and Guy. Won't they—'

'They, too, will get along quite well, I am thinking, without their *maître d'hôtel!*' laughed Robin. 'I can send them a wire at the hotel now, and ring up Jane and Guy later on and tell them what has happened. I am quite sure they would say I had done the right thing.'

'It – it would be lovely,' said Mariella longingly.

'Then it is settled,' said Robin. 'My car is in the car-park round the corner. Suppose we go there, and you get in and wait for me while I send the wire. By the way, what are you doing tonight? Have you arranged anything?'

'Not so far,' said Mariella. 'I expect we shall go to a

81

theatre – that is, if Nigel gets back in time. When he meets one of his friends and gets talking about horses, he forgets everything,' she added ruefully.

'I suspected that!' laughed Robin. 'Good-bye for the present, then. I shall not be long.'

In just over ten minutes he was back again. Although he was so big and quiet and slow-spoken, he could certainly get things done, thought Mariella, as he placed a parcel carefully on the back seat and slid behind the steering-wheel.

'I got us some "packed lunch",' he said, 'but I am thinking that we shall have to unpack it, so as to get it into my pockets!'

They drove out of the car park into Princes Street, turned off past the Mound, and entered Edinburgh's historic High Street. The castle towered above them on its rock and, clinging to its skirts, rose the tall 'landes', the tenement houses which, huddling together in picturesque disorder, made up the Old Town, that climbed like a scaly lizard up to the very foot of the castle. As they drove down towards the Canongate, history closed in upon them. The crazy-roofed old houses on either side were cleft by narrow 'wyndes', which disclosed the remains of gardens, and on the walls of the alleys you could read many a historic name. Sometimes, between the houses, you caught an unexpected view of mountain or distant hills.

They drove down past the old Tolbooth, and so out into the broad square outside the Palace of Holyroodhouse. Here they parked the car, and strode on foot towards the King's Park. Above them they could see the dark lion's profile of Arthur's Seat silhouetted against the blue sky, and below it, the Salisbury Crags. A building on the left caught Mariella's attention, the McCreedy Livery Stables.

'That's where Nigel has gone,' she said. Through an archway they saw a bandy-legged figure in riding breeches with a couple of stable-boys in attendance. 'And *that* will be Jock O'Dowd! Quick, Robin! We don't want to be seen!'

They hurried onwards, feeling like a couple of conspirators. As they climbed the stony pathway Edinburgh fell away at their feet.

'It must be lovely up here at night,' said Mariella, when they paused for a moment to get their breath and to admire the view.

'It is indeed very beautiful,' answered Robin, quietly, but Mariella could hear in his soft voice the pride every Scot feels for his splendid capital. 'The Old Town is like a jewelled snake, and the bridges are chains of topaz flung across the chasm between old and new!'

They had lunch on the top of Arthur's Seat. Out of one of Robin's capacious pockets came sandwiches, shortbread, and fruit. Out of the other, a bottle of orange squash. The larks were singing in the warm June sunshine, and all around them were the most wonderful views.

'There's the sea!' cried Mariella. 'It must be the Firth of Forth. Oh, how blue it is! And look at all the mountains!'

'Yes, it is a good day to be seeing the mountains,' said Robin. 'Away to the west, there is Ben Cleuch and Ben Vorlich. To the east, Ben Ledi. One can even see Schiehallion – over there, can you see, between Loch Rannoch and Loch Tummel? He must be at least sixty miles away! And, yes, one can see Dark Lochnager, to the east of Braemar. He must be at a distance of nearly seventy miles! We are indeed lucky! Now look over there – that is Ben Lomond, and the other one is Ben More, near the Braes of Balquhidder.'

'In another moment you'll be having me as crazy about mountains as Jane and Guy!' laughed Mariella. 'They're so remote, and blue, and mysterious, it makes me want to climb them! Just think, at this very moment Guy and Jane may be sitting on the top of Ben Cruachan over there.'

'No, over *there!*' corrected Robin solemnly, and, putting his hands on Mariella's shoulders, he turned her round a little. 'Yes, as you say, they are probably at this moment looking out over Oban and the harbour, away to the Hebrides. Or they may be looking down on Loch Awe with its many little islands – on Kilchurn Castle—'

'You love your home?' said Mariella. For one mad moment she had thought of leaning back against Robin and putting her head on his shoulder. He was so kind, and strong, and dependable. But she resisted the temptation. There was only one person's shoulder she wanted to rest upon, and he wasn't here.

'Oh, yes,' Robin said in answer to her question. 'I am loving my home very dearly.'

'Then didn't it hurt to see it turned into a hotel?' she asked.

'Och, no! Now I am sharing my beautiful home with people less fortunate.'

'That's a grand way to look at it!' said Mariella. 'All the same, I think you're generous, Robin. If it were me, I think I'd want to keep it all to myself. No trippers for me!'

'Och, but you do not get trippers at Allt nan Ros,' he assured her. 'The people who come there are those who really love the place.'

They stayed on top of the mountain until the sun began to go down; then they descended at a run. Robin produced a box of chocolates, and Mariella, happily munching chocolate cracknels, thought she had never had such a lovely, peaceful day. She was one of those people who are content with simple pleasures. A day out in the open air with the sun shining, and someone to talk to – that was Mariella's idea of happiness!

They had tea in the Royal Botanical Gardens on the far

84

side of Edinburgh, and were back again at Mrs McDougal's soon after six. They found that Nigel had come in only a few minutes before. When he saw Robin his eyebrows lifted.

'Oh, hullo, Campbell! I thought you were in Dalmally?'

'I am changing my plans at the last moment,' answered Robin. 'I am meeting Mariella and am taking her up Arthur's Seat instead.'

Nigel didn't look too pleased at this statement. To tell the truth, he wasn't feeling in a very good temper. The mare he had gone to see hadn't come up to Jock's description, or to Nigel's expectations. He had bought her, however, and now had an unpleasant feeling that he had been done.

'Oh, I see,' he said. 'Well, if you'd only *told* me you wanted to go up there all that much, Mariella, I'd have put Jock off. You had only to say, you know.'

'Oh, it was quite all right,' answered Mariella. 'We had a beautiful day, didn't we, Robin, and it would have been such a pity for you to miss Jock.'

'Might have been better if I had!' grumbled Nigel.

'By the way, Monkhouse,' put in Robin. 'Had you arranged anything for this evening?'

'Hadn't thought about it until this moment,' confessed Nigel. 'I suppose it will be a theatre. Done anything about it, Mariella, old girl?'

Before Mariella could reply, Robin said quickly: 'While you were waiting for me in the car, Mariella, I am taking the liberty of booking seats for us all at the Lyceum Theatre. I got almost the only seats left.'

'Oh, Robin, how perfectly wonderful!' exclaimed Mariella. 'The Lyceum? That's where *Quality Street* is, isn't it? I've been longing to see it.'

Even Nigel looked pleased. Since Robin had booked the seats all on his own, he would presumably be paying for them. Nigel was never averse to a theatre at someone else's expense.

'We have just time for a meal,' said Robin, 'and for Mariella to put on a pretty frock. You see, I am knowing something about women! And while the meal is cooking – I am assured by Mrs McDougal that it will be only perhaps a quarter of an hour or so – I could be ringing up Guy and Jane at the Allt nan Ros. They will be back by now. Would you like to speak to them, Mariella?'

'Oh, please,' said Mariella. 'Give me a call when you've finished, Robin. I'll wait in here. Do you know where the phone is?'

'Oh, yes – I am seeing it in the hall.'

He strode out, and Mariella went over to the window. Arthur's Seat was bathed in the evening sunlight. It was odd to think that only a few short hours ago she had been up there, looking out over the blue hills.

'Well, now I've bought the mare,' Nigel was saying, 'suppose you come down to the school and say what you think of her. What about tomorrow morning?'

Once upon a time – in fact, only yesterday – Mariella would have been thrilled at the idea of Nigel consulting her. Now, funnily enough, she wasn't.

'Oh, not tomorrow morning,' she said. 'It's Sunday, and we'd arranged to go to St Giles. Remember?'

'Oh, had we? Can't say I do. Very well, afternoon then?'

'I might come in the afternoon,' Mariella said cautiously.

'You don't seem mad keen—'

Fortunately Robin's voice broke in upon them at this moment.

'Mariella! It is your turn! Jane says she is longing to speak to you. And, by the way,' he added, as she took up the receiver, 'I have reversed the charge, so you can have as long as you like. It is on the hotel!'

'Oh, thank you, Robin,' Mariella said gratefully. 'That was very thoughtful of you. . . Hullo, Jane! This is

86

Mariella.'

'Oh, Mariella – we had such a splendid climb,' said the voice at the other end. 'You have no idea how beautiful it was on top of Cruachan—'

'Oh, yes, I have,' broke in Mariella, 'because Robin and I were on top of Arthur's Seat this afternoon! It was beautiful there, too, and so clear we could see all the mountains for miles round. Robin told me all their names, but I'm afraid I can't remember them now!'

'I wish we'd known you were up there,' said Jane. 'You'd have seemed so much nearer! Oh, and Mariella – Guy and I are officially engaged, and you're the first to know it! . . . Yes, Guy put on my engagement ring on the top of Cruachan, beside those wickedly dangerous-looking crags on the north side! You should see my ring, Mariella. It's a family heirloom, and it's a glorious fire-opal surrounded by diamonds. I'm just longing to show it to you!'

'I'll see it tomorrow,' said Mariella. 'Good-bye, Jane, and love to dear Guy, and my congratulations and best wishes to you both. See you tomorrow!' Although, as Robin had said, the call was 'on the hotel', yet it *was* long-distance, and Robin would pay for it in the end because he owned the Allt nan Ros, so she mustn't take advantage of his generosity. So argued Mariella as she put down the instrument firmly.

The weekend sped away like a flash as weekends do when they are filled to the brim with exciting things. First, there was church, sitting between Nigel and Robin. Then there was their reunion with Jane and Guy – now properly engaged, as Jane said.

'I hope not *im*properly before!' teased Guy.

'Well, you know what I mean. My ring and everything! Look, Mariella, isn't it beautiful?' She held out her hand for Mariella to see her ring for the sixth time at least. No engaged girl could have been prouder or happier than Jane at that moment!

In the evening there was a concert, and then they all went with Jane and Guy to the Trossachs Hotel for coffee. Jane went to bed early so as to be ready for her performance the following evening, but the rest of them sat talking till nearly midnight.

On the Monday night they all went to the Empire Theatre (Upper Circle) to see Jane dance the leading female role in *Donald of the Burthens*.

'Oh, the lovely music!' exclaimed Mariella. 'I adore Scottish music!'

'Do you see how they have managed to bring in the pipes?' asked Robin. 'I mean, how they have managed to get them in without the usual drone at the beginning?'

'No, now you come to mention it, how do they?'

'All the rest of the orchestra plays "F" madly until he's in and that drowns it!' laughed Robin. 'There is, of course, only the one piper.'

They all left Edinburgh on the Tuesday – except, of course Mariella, who stayed on until the end of term proper, which was the following Friday.

When they had finished breakfast Robin brought up the matter of paying for their rooms, and Mariella heaved a sigh of relief.

'We have a lot of settling up to do,' he said. 'There are the ballet tickets to pay for, and our rooms here. Will you be telling us, Mariella, how much it is that we are owing you, and Monkhouse and I will repay you.'

Mariella named the sum, and Robin took his wallet out of his pocket.

'It seems a very little for so much pleasure,' he said, with a smile. 'You are sure that is all?'

'Quite sure,' answered Mariella.

'Look, Mariella!' exclaimed Nigel, 'I haven't a spot of loose cash on me. I'll settle up with you when you come home next week. You won't be wanting it all that badly.'

'That is quite all right,' put in Robin Campbell quietly. 'I am paying Mariella myself. That is correct, is it not?' He took out his wallet again.

'Quite correct,' said the girl, 'but ought you—'

'Monkhouse will give me a cheque,' said Robin. 'That is all right, is it not, Monkhouse?'

'Oh, yes – of course,' said Nigel, looking a little taken aback. 'Want it now?'

'Please,' said Himself of Inveross, with a slight bow. He really was the politest person, thought Mariella. Meanwhile he stood waiting.

Nigel took out his cheque-book, and made out a cheque without a word, while Mariella watched him, amazed. It was easy, it seemed, to manage Nigel – if only you knew how! If it had been her, he'd have left his cheque-book at home, too!

When they had gone she put the money away with a silent prayer of thankfulness to Robin Campbell, but that night she cried herself to sleep. It was awful to be forced to realize that Robin possessed qualities – strict honesty, for one – that Nigel lacked. Of course, she told herself firmly, Nigel had other qualities, and he was much more handsome than Robin. In fact, you couldn't call Robin handsome at all. Not even good-looking, though he was so big and tall. But he was nice and kind, and he did *consider* people. He was the sort of person you could turn to if you were in trouble, thought Mariella. She was growing quite fond of Robin!

Chapter 6

Television Party

The Sordys were full of excitement! Me Mam had bought a television set – on the 'never-never', of course! Couldn't afford to pay for it on the nail. Still, the television was the Sordys' as long as Me Mam kept up the payments. And now it was imperative that the Sordys had a television party. When the children set off for school that morning, Me Mam gave them their orders.

'Tak the string bag, Ella – no, it had better be our Lily. Our Ella'd leave it in the school cloakroom like as not! – and get two pound of cooked ham from the shop on yer way from school. And mind you see they cut it thin, or it'll not go round. Here's a basket, D'reen. You get two dozen sausage-rolls, and one of them ice-cream bricks that'll last two hours. And mind you come straight home wi' it, or it'll melt wi' yer hot hands. And ye'd better get a dozen of them cream buns at Allgoods in Front Street. The ones wi' the coconut icing on top and cream inside. Now don't you go forgettin' nothin'! . . . Wait a minute! You haven't got no money.' She thrust an old leather purse into D'reen's hands; and with a final: 'Don't you go leavin' it in no cloakroom, mind!' she pushed her out into the street and shut the door. At last she'd got rid of the kids for a bit!

At eight o'clock that night the television party was in full swing. Most of the furniture had been moved out of the Room into the living-room – horsehair sofa, two armchairs, and two smalls. The bamboo table, denuded of its plant, made an excellent cake-stand, and was heaped with sausage-rolls and sandwiches. The television set occupied the place of honour underneath Grandpa Sordy's critical, and, one couldn't help feeling, disapproving gaze. Goings-on like this had never taken place in *his* house said his fierce grey eyes! Royalty, on the other hand, looked down in silent and smiling benediction on the guests – Mrs Rickerby, Mrs Dickson-from-next-door, Mrs Duffy-round-the-corner, and Mrs Pratt-of-the-shop.

The knob was turned! The moment had come!

'Ministers arrive for peace conference in Geneva,' said the voice of the announcer (close-up of several bald-headed gentlemen walking in dignified procession up a flight of marble steps)... 'Duke of Avon lays foundation-stone of Bradley's new town hall' (close-up of yet another bald-headed gentleman, trowel in hand)... 'My! Who would think he were a reel dook! It all goes to show ... what's he doin' now? ... Shut up, our Lily! We can't hear nothin'... Down to the sea in ships! Marchioness of Castle-town christens Britain's newest liner *Marchioness of Castle-town* ... There she goes! Oh, beautiful launch!' (close-up of both marchionesses)... 'Sir Aga Singh arrives by air to attend Royal garden party' (close-up of large, dark gentleman in a turban, being disgorged out of an aeroplane)... 'Our cameraman takes a stroll in Regent's Park and greets a small friend' (picture of well-known television personality feeding a small squirrel perched on his shoulder). Chorus of 'oos' and 'ahs' from the younger members of the Sordy family. Little shriek from Mrs Sordy: 'Ow! It makes me feel tickly! So reel-like! ... Well, that's the end of the noos. Let's have a look at the *Radio Times*. Yes, that's it you're sittin' on, Lily... Afraid there's nothin' reelly good on tonight – like a v'riety-show. It's just a concert by the BBC Sym-pony Orchestra. Terrible highbrow! *Swan Lake* or summat. It's by somebody strange – a canna pernoonce his name. Sounds like sneezin' to me!'

'Oh, look!' put in Mrs Dickson, with a squeal of excitement. 'There's a note aboot it here. It says the conductor is Sebastian Scott – that's the one that's married to Miss Weston. They live at Bracken Hall, near where our Harriet works. It says: "Owing to circumstances beyond our control" (that's the babby!) "Miss Weston will not be able to dance the Solo in this famous ballet, so we are using a film that was taken some months ago instead." '

'Oh, well – we can hae oor supper while it's on,' said Mrs Sordy, 'and hope for summat a bit more peppy a'terwards. Mind oot the way, Lily, and let us past to mak the cocoa! . . .'

The television supper was well under way by the time the film of Veronica Weston in Solo from *Lac des Cygnes* was announced. The Sordy family and their friends were chattering noisily, stirring their cocoa, and making short work of the plates of sliced ham and potato crisps. The cream buns were being kept for later on in the evening. Only Ella sat silent, watching the white, dancing figure on the screen. So this was Veronica Weston! This dark-eyed dancer, moving so gracefully, so effortlessly it was hard to believe she was real! Oh, lovely, lovely Veronica Weston!

Suddenly a popping noise sounded outside in the street and the television screen was rent as if by lightning.

'Ow!' giggled Mrs Rickerby. 'It's a proper snowstorm, ain't it!'

'It's not a snowstorm. It's your Alfred!' exclaimed Mrs Sordy in outraged fury. 'Your Alfred and his dratted motorbike! He oughta be ashamed of hisself – goin' aboot wi'oot no suppressor on!'

'Well, why should our Alfred pay to be suppressed?' demanded Mrs Rickerby. 'Just for other folk's pleasure. Right's right!'

'*Some* folks thinks of other folk besides theirsels,' said

Mrs Sordy tartly, 'but not your Alfred!'

'Our Alfred is as good a lad as ever lived,' exclaimed Mrs Rickerby. 'But why should our Alfred—'

'Oh, shut up, do!' exclaimed Mrs Duffy. 'Look it's gone right. Ain't she pretty, now?'

'Not so bad,' agreed Mrs Pratt. 'I like a few more spangles mesel', though – like in the panto. My goodness! What's wrong, noo?'

The television screen had become convulsed. Rows of Veronica Westons careered across the stage in mad *fouettés*, as many-headed as the mythical Hydra! Snow poured down upon her! She disappeared altogether only to emerge from the snowdrift like a figure in plaster of Paris.

'It's your Sid and his Consul!' snorted Mrs Rickerby triumphantly. 'What about *'im* being suppressed for a change? What aboot 'im?'

The screen returned to normal, Sid Sordy evidently having switched off his engine. The door opened and two visitors stood on the threshold – Sid in a loud, check suit, and Gloria in black satin, with a fur coat slung casually round her shoulders.

'Hullo, ducks!' said Gloria Sordy. 'We've come to 'ave a look-in. Any supper goin'?'

'We might find you a sausage-roll and some crisps,' said Mrs Sordy. 'The 'am's finished.'

'OK,' said Gloria. 'Just something to nibble'll do. We've had our high tea. Gosh! Not too bad, is it?' She sank down in the chair her mother-in-law pulled forward like a wet, black seal.

'That's a new coat, ain't it, Glor?' said Mrs Sordy, pleased to show off her opulent daughter-in-law to the neighbours. 'Ain't seen it afore, 'ave I?'

'Not as I knows of, dear,' said Gloria. 'Only got it last week.'

'Coney, ain't it?' said Mrs Rickerby.

'Not on your life! Canadian squirrel if *you* please. Cost over four hundred quid!'

There was an awe-stricken silence for a few minutes. Then Gloria became aware that Ella was staring at her coat with a queer, fixed expression on her small face. She mistook it for admiration.

'What's the matter, kid? Didn't you never see a fur coat afore? Like to stroke it?'

To her surprise, Ella shrank away.

'You mean – you mean your coat's made of little squirrels – like the one in the pit'cher?'

'Well, I haven't seen the picture – maybe that was before Sid and me come in, but this coat is made of squirrel all right, if that's what you're getting at. It's no cheap imitation, I assure you!'

'*Hundreds* of squirrels?' pursued Ella. 'Hundreds?'

'Hven't counted 'em!' said Gloria sarcastically. 'Like to have a go, yourself?' Then, at last, something in the child's expression struck her. 'Hey, Mam! What's the matter with this kid? Has she gone daft?'

Ella had, in fact, turned her back on the party and run from the room, the tears streaming down her face. Gloria wearing a coat made out of the dead bodies of hundreds of squirrels! Little, tame, confiding squirrels like the one sitting on the cameraman's shoulder on the television! Gentle little squirrels! Not for the first time, Ella had come up against one of the cruelties inflicted upon animals by human beings, and her heart rebelled. Why should it be? Who allowed it? Why should people like Sid's Gloria clothe their bodies in the skins of pretty little squirrels who had never done anyone any harm? She determined to ask Mr Roebottom, the vicar, next time she saw him, or better still, Timothy. Timothy, she felt, might know the answer.

Chapter 7

The Summer Show

Never had there been such a dress! It was the dress every budding dancer dreams of – the bodice darted, tucked, and softly folded until it fitted the figure like the sepals enclosing a flower-bud. From the taut waistline, it flowed out, layer upon layer of crisp, grey net, over stiff, white tarletan. It was cut jagged at the hem to suggest rags – but only a mere suggestion, mind you! It was a classical ballet dress, so it must still be beautiful!

'Why, Ella,' exclaimed the beauty-loving Miss Jones, 'you've got a lovely figure!'

Ella blushed. Miss Jones had had a hard job in the first place to persuade her to take off her clothes and stand there 'in the altogether', as Ella put it, in the presence of another human being – even a dressmaker!

'Me Mam says it's not decent,' she explained.

'But, Ella – I'm a woman, just like your mam,' said poor Miss Jones, standing with the frock over her arm. 'Surely you don't think it's indecent to take off your clothes in front of your mother, do you?'

'I never does,' said Ella. 'Not since I was a babby.'

'But you must take off your clothes *sometime*,' argued Miss Jones. 'What about when you go to bed?'

'I sleeps in me vest,' said Ella, 'and so does our Lily, and our D'reen.'

'Well, when you have a bath, then?'

'I gets into me bath with me vest on, tucked up, and then I takes it off,' said Ella, 'just afore I gets into the water. 'Sides there ain't no one there.'

'Oh—'

They looked at each other. It seemed an impasse.

'Well, I'm afraid you will have to get used to taking off your clothes if you're going to be a dancer,' declared Miss Jones. 'You see, a ballet dress fits so beautifully that it just *won't* go on top of your other clothes. It's made that way. You've just *got* to take everything off before you can put it on.'

Ballet won. Ella had given in, and hence the remark about the figure. It was quite true – the child *had* a lovely figure – slender, small-boned, elegant – though nobody would have guessed it under the clothes she wore! Most of Ella's clothes came from the Parish jumble sale, and those that didn't were handed down from Our Lil, or Our D'reen who, as we have said, were both a great deal bigger than Ella, though they *were* younger.

Ella's skirts were usually Mrs Phillipson's, cut down by Mrs Duffy-round-the-corner, who plied a sewing machine as well as home-perm curlers, and who 'cut down' and 'made over' clothes for a small amount. She 'made over' Mrs Phillipson's skirt for Ella by cutting a foot or so off the hem, pleating the waistband at regular intervals, and running a large and wavy pleat down the centre back.

Ella's underclothes usually came from the jumble, too. Her vests differed in that they were sometimes so long that they came down past her knees and made a lump inside her pants and sometimes so short and 'felted', they merely reached the middle of her tummy, so that there was a large and draughty gap between the place where the vest ended and where the panties began.

If Ella's underwear was a sample of what the other little girls in Pit Street wore, it was no wonder they didn't like undressing in public!

And now it was the day of the Summer Show – the long-awaited Saturday when the entire Mary Martin School of Ballet (reinforced with some twenty pupils from Blackheath) showed their skill in the art of dancing in its broadest terms. All kinds of dancing – from tap to classical ballet – was to be shown. The matinée began by the youngest pupils – babies of three and four – showing off their limbering-up exercises. Veronica Weston sat in the stage-box, between her husband, Sebastian Scott, and her forming dancing mistress, Mary Martin, and tried hard not to yawn. She knew she oughtn't to yawn, that these exercises were doing the children lots of good – even if they would never make actual dancers of them. She knew that the Mary Martin School was doing a wonderful job with these children. Still, forty pairs of legs in black tights pretending to be bicycles – it was hypnotizing! . . . Ah, this was the end of the limbering. Good! Some real ballet, at last! But only here and there in this beautifully dressed, beautifully trained, school did Veronica, with her practised eye, see the signs of outstanding grace and talent. A little girl called Mavis Hunter danced a simplified *Sugar Plum Fairy*, and did it beautifully. She was going up to the Wells next year, whispered Mary. Two children did a Dutch Dance exceedingly well, but in a rather 'mannered' style. They would do well in pantomime later on, thought Veronica. 'They'll be in it next Christmas,' Mary told her. 'They're older than they look!' A lovely girl in an ankle-length ballet dress danced the waltz from *Les Sylphides*. Her arms were graceful and expressive, her head and shoulders beautiful. Veronica turned to Mary with raised eyebrows. . . 'Oh, yes,' whispered Mary. 'She's lovely, isn't she? She's just come *back* from the Wells. Her thighs are too big. Poor Cynthia! They've tried everything, but it was no use at all. In a long dress, she's perfect. Such a pity!'

And now it was getting near the end of the Show. The prizes had been presented, the certificates handed over.

The members of the audience had clapped their hands sore, as their darlings dipped in perfectly trained curtsies before the famous Veronica Weston, who had left her box and was now on the stage where a small table, covered with black velvet and heaped with prizes, now stood. A bouquet of deep pink roses and carnations had been handed to the ballerina, and now she was back in her box, waiting for the curtain to rise on the last two items.

'The Fairy-tale Book,' she said, turning to her programme. Then, before she had time to read the names of the dancers, the curtain rose. At the back of the stage stood a large, brightly coloured picture-book. As the audience watched, the leaves opened, and out stepped two fairy-tale characters – Dick Whittington and his Cat. To music, faintly reminiscent of Tchaikovsky's 'White Cat' music in *The Sleeping Beauty*, they did their *pas-de-deux* and retired to the back of the stage. Again the leaves opened, and out came Jack and Jill, followed by Beauty and the Beast. Then appeared Little Miss Muffet, who raised a laugh with her spider. And then . . .

'*Mary!*' said Veronica, after watching Cinderella for just one minute. 'Mary, who is that child?'

Mary Martin smiled the funny little smile that Veronica knew well. She only smiled like that when she had something up her sleeve!

'I was wondering if you'd notice her,' said Mary Martin. 'She's quite lovely, isn't she?'

'She's beautiful!' said Veronica, dreamily, of plain little Ella Sordy. 'Beautiful! The way she walks. The expression on her face. Her lovely arms. Her hands. Her supple, arched feet. Who on earth is she?'

'I'll tell you about her in a minute,' promised Mary Martin. 'She has only learnt ballet for a few months. She hadn't danced a step when I took her into my Blackheath class last Christmas.'

'Ah, that accounts for it,' put in Sebastian, who was sitting astride a gilt chair a little behind the two of them. 'You had her all to yourself, dear Mary, so she has had the best chance possible!'

'What a sweet thing to say, Sebastian!' laughed Mary Martin. 'I do hope it's true! Well, this is the end of the "Fairy-tale Book". Now, before the next thing begins – it's the last, by the way – let me tell you a little about Ella Sordy. . .'

When she had finished, Veronica looked grave.

'Then she's nearly thirteen? Older than she looks. Something must be done quickly, or it will be too late. She ought to be having daily classes. Can't you take her on, Mary? If it's a matter of money—'

'It's not as simple as that,' Mary told her. 'You see, there is her family.' Briefly Mary Martin sketched in a picture of Pit Street and the Sordy family – Our Lily, Our D'reen, the red-armed, coarse Mrs Sordy, the squalid atmosphere. 'It wouldn't matter about their being *poor*,' she ended. 'In fact it wouldn't matter where they lived – there are plenty of families in pit cottages who would know how to foster a child like Ella. Mere poverty is nothing. But the Sordys! You'd understand if you saw them. There's a complete lack of cultural background – so important to a girl of Ella's age. Nothing for her to read except comics. Nothing to watch except television, and only what Ella's mam calls "peppy stuff" allowed on that. Any decent music or dancing is switched off! No pictures, no books no beauty of any sort. Even if I got her over here for a class or two, say on a Saturday (during the week would be impossible because of her school) – what good would it do? She would go back to her family and Pit Street!'

'Yes, it's certainly a problem,' agreed Veronica. 'I don't quite know how to tackle it—'

'But *I do!*' broke in Sebastian so loudly that they both

jumped, and the people in the adjoining box stared at them in disapproval. They were interrupting the Musical Comedy number, and their little Rosalind was in it! 'We'll give her a scholarship!'

'Which scholarship, darling, and where to?' Veronica asked her husband.

'Ours,' pronounced Sebastian. 'The Scott-Weston Exhibition. I've just invented it! It will take the form of a year's tuition at Sadler's Wells School – board and lodging paid for at the Lady Bailey Home for Dancers – and an extension to cover further training, if the holder proves a winner! Well, how about it?'

'It sounds just what is wanted,' said Veronica. 'Why didn't I think of it myself!'

'You haven't the common business sense of yours truly,' declared Sebastian. 'Never had, my dear! To continue – we'll give the first chance to this kid – Ella Sordy. If *you* recommend her, my darling, the Wells will jump at her!'

'I suppose they will,' agreed Veronica. Although *prima ballerina assoluta* of the world's most famous company, she was still very modest, and never 'threw her weight about'.

'All that remains, then, is to tell the redoubtable Mrs Sordy, Ella's mam, about the scheme, and whisk Ella off to the Wells by the next train,' went on Sebastian.

'You leave that to me,' said Mary Martin. 'I'll go and see her. I'll enjoy doing it!'

How is it that things that seem easy always prove to be difficult in the extreme? You would have thought no one – least of all Mrs Sordy – could possibly object to Ella being presented with an all-in scholarship to the most famous dancing school in the world. For the next five years (in all likelihood) Ella would be completely provided for – food, clothes – yes, Miss Weston had hinted that she would at least provide the child with her first outfit, and all her dancing things – in fact, everything had been thought of. All Ella's mam would have to do would be to feed her daughter during the holidays. No, on second thoughts – she probably wouldn't come home for the holidays.

But what Miss Martin didn't know – and what Mrs Sordy wasn't telling her – was that Ella was *not* her daughter. She got paid a sum weekly for Ella, and another sum quarterly for Ella's clothes and other expenses. In short, she was a considerable amount into pocket with Ella, and she couldn't afford to lose her. Of course, she *could* take another baby from the Cottage Homes, she supposed. But think of the bother! She was a bit too old, now, to start messing about with babies, and Ella was getting to be quite useful. Besides, in a couple of years' time Ella could get a job and then she'd be able to send her old mam a tidy bit of her earnings. And she would, too! Me Mam had brought Ella up to know what was right and proper! She was a good girl, was our Ella. Me Mam was getting fonder of Ella every minute!

'No,' she told the astounded Miss Martin, 'I don't 'old wi' them carryings on – the stage, and that. Our Ella's been brought up proper. She'll go out to work, like our Lily and our D'reen.'

'You do realize, don't you, Mrs Sordy,' said Mary in desperation, 'that you may be stopping Ella from becoming one of the world's greatest dancers?'

'Oh, get along!' said Mrs Sordy, in sheer unbelief. 'Our Ella!'

Chapter 8

The Circus Baby

Mary Martin found occasion to go over to Blackheath to supervise her ballet class upon more than one occasion during the next couple of months. Sometimes her excuse was one thing, sometimes another. Her real reason, however, was to watch little Ella Sordy, and note her progress. Although she realized by now that Ella was lost to the art of ballet, yet she couldn't help being interested in her. The child went ahead by leaps and bounds. She had left behind her the period of awkwardness that every child goes through, when first she begins to learn the difficult and, yes, unnatural art of ballet, for no one can deny that the exaggerated, 'turned out' position of classical ballet *is* unnatural, however beautiful it may look to the trained eye.

Besides learning the actual steps and positions about ten times as quickly as any ordinary pupil, Ella obviously delighted in what she was doing. In fact, it was quite plain to Mary Martin that the child lived for it. Thus Mary's heart was heavy, for it is indeed a sad thing for a mistress to watch a pupil's talent being wasted. Here was Ella being offered the chance of a life-time and, just because she had a stiff-necked mother, she couldn't take it. Miss Martin discussed Ella's Mam at length with her assistant, June Robinson.

'I don't wish Ella's wretched mam any harm, June,' she said, 'but if she *did* happen to fall off a pair of steps and break her neck—'

June burst out laughing.

'You sound most ferocious, Mary! I believe you're serious!'

'I never was more serious in my life, my dear,' Mary assured her. 'Unfortunately, I don't suppose it's the least likely to happen!'

One hot Thursday towards the end of August, just before the dancing school went back, Mary parked her little car outside the hideous black and yellow façade of Blackheath Vicarage, and was ushered into the vicar's study by Mrs Carter, the woman who cleaned for the Roebottoms two days a week. Cynthia Roebottom came to meet her with a welcoming smile. They had become great friends since the ballet classes had started in Blackheath.

'Oh, hullo, Mary! How nice to see you! You're just in time for a cup of tea. I'm expecting the vicar back any minute. Do sit down.'

Mary sat down in the old leather armchair that Mrs Roebottom drew forward, and accepted the proffered cup of tea gratefully.

'Oh, thank you, she said. 'I can't refuse it on such a hot day! As a matter of fact, I came along to see your husband about the church hall for this next term. I suppose it's all right if I have it again? There are even more children coming than before!'

'You've no idea how interesting I've found these ballet classes,' said Cynthia, pouring out a cup of tea for herself and passing a plate of sandwiches to Mary. 'I'm a great lover of ballet, you know, though of course I can't often afford to go to see it. It's given me a great thrill to watch these children growing more graceful with every class—'

'Yes, it *is* gratifying, isn't it?' agreed Mary.

'I often go in and watch them,' went on Mrs Roebottom. There's one child – one little girl—'

'Yes?' prompted Mary.

'Ella Sordy, her name is,' said Cynthia (as if Mary didn't know!). 'She's quite lovely to watch. Oh, she's not pretty to look at – in fact, I suppose she's really quite plain, but you forget it when she moves. Even when she does the ugliest exercises – like those knee-bends—'

'*Pliés*,' said Mary.

'Yes, *pliés*. Well, when Ella does them, they actually look beautiful. Then there are the positions of the arms – *ports des bras*, I think you call them – they're usually so stiff when children do them at first, but Ella – well, in short, the child fascinates me. There's no other word for it! I just can't help watching her! I'm a bit of an artist, you know,' she added, the pink colour creeping into her thin cheeks. 'Nothing professional, of course, but I love drawing children. I always have, and really I've done some quite nice studies of Ella Sordy. I'm seriously thinking of sending them up to some publisher to see if they would do for book illustration. Would you like to see them?' She made a long arm over Mary's knee, opened the top drawer of a bureau and produced a sketchbook.

Mary took the book, and there before her was Ella – plain little Ella Sordy, plain no longer because of her extraordinary grace – Ella in the most enchanting positions – posing in *attitude grec, arabesque fondu*, Ella with arms quietly crossed in front of her, one foot posed behind her, standing like a Narcissus gazing into some forest pool. Ella leaping across the floor in *grands jetés*, light as a piece of thistledown, her plain little face, with the enormous dark eyes lit up with some hidden emotion that made her face plain no longer.

'Why, they're *lovely!*' said Mary Martin sincerely. 'I had no idea you had such talent!'

'Well, I certainly never knew I could draw so well,' confessed Mrs Roebottom. 'It's that child – there's something about her—'

'Everyone feels that,' said Mary. 'It's a great tragedy.'

'*What* is a great tragedy, if I may not seem too inquisitive?' said a warm, deep voice from the door – the vicar's voice.

'Oh, hullo, Mr Roebottom. We were just talking about little Ella Sordy. I was about to tell Cynthia what a tragedy it is that the child can't take advantage of the scholarship to Sadler's Wells School.'

'You mean she's really been offered one? Then *why* can't she take it?' demanded the vicar. 'I should say myself it would be a godsend. Get her out of that Sordy family. I have nothing actually against them, of course, but they're a bit rough and ready for a child like Ella, I've always thought.'

'We all think that, Mr Roebottom,' said Mary. 'Miss Weston – that is Veronica Weston, the ballerina, you know – was so struck by Ella's dancing that she and her husband immediately offered to give the child a scholarship to Sadler's Wells, but, as I was saying, Ella's mother won't consider it.'

'So *that's* what's making the poor mite so miserable!' exclaimed Mrs Roebottom. 'I've been wondering about it. You catch a child's moods when you draw her as I've drawn Ella. All the summer holidays – though she's practised by herself every day – I've known she was unhappy about something. But why should Mrs Sordy hold out against such an amazingly generous offer?'

'She talks about Ella going out to work like her other children,' explained Miss Martin. 'I suppose she thinks—'

'Ah, yes – I see it now!' broke in Mr Roebottom. 'She thinks that Our Ella'll go out to work and help keep her old mam for the rest of her feckless, lazy days!' His imitation of Our Mam was so perfect that Mary Martin burst out laughing. 'I know her little ways! Well, I shall proceed, here and now, to put a nice little spoke in Ella's mam's

105

wheel! You don't realize, I suppose, either of you, that our Mrs Sordy is not Ella's mam at all?'

His words stunned Mary Martin. She sat with the cup of tea in her hand, perfectly still, her mouth open. At last she stammered: 'Y-you mean that Ella is an *adopted* child?'

'No, I do *not*,' rapped out Mr Roebottom. 'If she were – legally adopted, that is – things might still be difficult. I mean that Ella was fostered, or whatever you call it, when an infant, by the Cottage Homes, and *that's* why Mam Sordy is digging in her claws. She gets – oh, I forget exactly how much, but it's a nice little sum, each week for Ella's keep, and another nice little sum quarterly for her clothes (which, by the way, our jumble sale provides!), and Ella's mam squanders the lot on fish and chips and comics!'

'Then – you mean—' faltered Mary, hardly daring to voice the thought that had come into her head.

'I mean that Mrs Sordy has no say at all about what Ella does for her living. The Board of Governors have sole authority over the child, and I don't fancy we'll have any trouble there. Why, Sir Giles Willington is a great friend of mine. Moreover, he's a rabid balletomane. He'll be thrilled to death to think of the Cottage Homes producing a ballerina!'

'Oh, Mr Roebottom, I don't know what to say,' said Mary. 'I don't know how to thank you.'

'Thank me? What on earth for?' demanded the vicar. 'Just for putting you straight about your facts? I wish everyone was as grateful! The things I do for some people and never get as much as the echo of a "thank you"!'

'It's really too amazing to be true,' went on Miss Martin. 'It's like a fairy-tale! I've been so very unhappy about the child. I remember my own childhood, you see, and how I longed and longed to be a dancer, but of course I couldn't. My figure stopped me. It must be ten times worse for Ella, because she must know she's good, and there's nothing to stop *her*. Nothing! Her figure's perfect.'

'Mary, you're a darling!' declared Cynthia Roebottom. 'It's no wonder you're such a splendid teacher. Why, I believe you're crying!'

'Only for happiness,' Mary Martin told her. 'You know, I've grown quite fond of the child.'

'So have I,' said Cynthia. 'I'll let you into a secret. All last spring – you remember that wickedly cold weather we had? – well I found out, quite by accident, that the poor child came straight from school, not only on Thursdays, but other days, too, and practised her ballet in the church hall. I rigged up an old oil stove to keep her warm, because of course it wouldn't have done to turn on the electric fires. In fact, between ourselves, it was all against regulations for her to use the hall at all, but *I* wasn't stopping her! Then I discovered that the mite went without any tea, so I took over some cocoa and a few sandwiches. That's when I've done most of my drawing.'

'God bless you, my dear,' said Mary. 'You may live to be proud of having helped to cherish little Ella Sordy!'

After the class that evening, Mary rang up Bracken Hall in Northumberland, where Veronica Weston and Sebastian Scott lived. She just couldn't wait another minute to tell them the great news! Sebastian answered the phone.

'Oh, hullo, Sebastian,' said Mary. 'This is Mary Martin. I've rung up about little Ella Sordy. Veronica isn't there, is she? . . . Oh, she's not. Well, never mind – as long as I tell *somebody*. Prepare for shocks! It appears that Ella's mam isn't her mam at all. No, you see she – Ella's mam – took Ella when she was a baby, as a foster child. She got paid by the Cottage Homes for looking after her. Her mother, it seems, was a dancer and bare-back rider in a circus that happened to be visiting Blackheath. She had an accident – Ella's real mother, I mean – and died in the

107

hospital when Ella was born. So *that's* where the child gets her dancing from. Funny, isn't it! Her father was a trapeze artist. He was Italian, by the way, so that accounts for Ella's colouring and huge, dark eyes. . . Yes, I thought you'd think so. The important thing now is that, as Mr Roebottom, the vicar here, says, Mrs Sordy has no power whatsoever to stop Ella from going to the Wells, or anywhere else, for that matter. It's all in the hands of the Board of Governors. Mr Roebottom says he knows Sir Giles Willington, and he assures me there will be no opposition from him. So, if you could . . . Oh, you will? Well, if you go and roust them round, I'm sure there'll be no difficulty. Better still, get Veronica to go. . . *What's* that you say? . . . Say it again, Sebastian! . . . I can't believe it! . . . Why didn't you tell me before! . . . A little girl! Oh, Sebastian – I'm so happy for you both!'

Having run nearly all the way to the telephone kiosk in her excitement, Mary now proceeded to run all the way back to the Vicarage again.

'Cynthia, Cynthia!' she called, when she got back to the house. 'I've just heard the most wonderful news! Veronica has had her baby – yes, a little girl, and her name is to be Victoria. Vicki, for short!'

Part Three

Chapter 1

Journey South

You remember those two trains I told you about at the beginning of this story? Well, we have caught up with them, and now you know a lot more about the little girl sitting in the corner of her third-class compartment. The two tears dropped off the end of her nose, and got caught by the curve of her upper lip. She licked them off surreptitiously and turned to her comic again. But even the hair-raising adventures of Detective Dan failed to hold her interest. Her thoughts kept wandering back to Pit Street, the colliery village she had left only that morning. She thought of her mam and dad, Lily, and D'reen. They would be back there now – all fast asleep. Lily and D'reen would have more room in the big bed, because she, Ella, would be missing, and tomorrow, when they went to school, there would be a vacant desk in Miss Fisher's class. She wondered if, when they called the register, they would forget and call out 'Ella Sordy'! Then there would be silence because she, Ella, was here on this great, rocking, racketing train, rushing on its headlong way to London!

They had all come to Newcastle to see her off. Me Mam had got over her chagrin at the loss of the extra money Ella brought in, and had kissed her, and told her to be 'a good girl', and Lily and D'reen had given her some chocolate and the comic. Even Sid and Gloria had turned up the previous evening to say 'Ta-ta'.

And if you think it odd for anyone's thoughts to go back to a place like Pit Street, remember that it was the only home Ella had ever known. Me Mam, raw-boned, loud-voiced, insensitive, was her mother to all intents and purposes. Lily and D'reen were her sisters.

'Oh, Mam! Mam!' sobbed Ella under her breath, and two more tears trickled slowly down her nose.

'What's the matter, dear?' asked an anxious-looking lady sitting in the corner opposite. 'Are you all by yourself?'

'Yes, miss,' said Ella, not knowing how pathetic and utterly forlorn she looked in the uncompromising glare of the roof-light.

'But surely you're very young to be going to London all by yourself? How old are you, dear?'

'I'm thirteen – near on fourteen,' answered Ella.

'Oh, you're older than you look. And where are you going to stay, dear? With relations? With your auntie, maybe?'

'I ain't got no ant-ie – leastways not i' London,' said Ella. 'I'm going to stay along of a Lady Bailey.'

Her questioner's eyes met those of a fellow-traveller. 'Going out to service, poor little thing,' said their glances.

'Well, you must try to give satisfaction,' said the large lady from the opposite seat.

'I'm sure I hope so, miss,' said Ella.

'And not break things,' added the other traveller.

'What sorta things should I break, miss?' asked Ella, turning to her.

'Well – cups, and saucers, and plates, and – and glasses, dear – the things you will have to wash.'

Ella stared at her. It suddenly dawned upon her what the woman meant. Lily or D'reen would have burst out

with: 'Don't be so soft! I ain't old enough to be no servant!'
But Ella was far too polite. She said gently – for, after all,
the two ladies were trying to be kind – 'I ain't a-going to
wash no dishes. I'm a-going to dance.'

The women's faces were a study.

'Dance? You mean—'

'I'm a-going to Sadler's Wells,' said Ella, 'to learn to
dance like Veronica Weston, and this Lady Bailey is my
digs.'

'*Well!*' said the two women in unison.

After this, the compartment settled down to sleep.
Someone turned down the light to a ghostly blue glare; the
air got thicker and hotter; the whirring of the wheels, the
grinding of the couplings, the roar of tunnels, the screech
of other trains met and passed in an instant, wove themselves into a sort of mad lullaby. A large businessman sitting
on the seat opposite, next to the talkative lady, dropped his
head on his vast chest, and snored. A fresh-faced soldier,
next to Ella, snuggled down into his army greatcoat and
stretched out his long legs. Then drew them back again
apologetically, as they came into contact with the talkative
lady's high-heeled shoes. The train fled south through the
night, eating up the miles like some great prehistoric
monster of fire and smoke, taking small Ella Sordy further
and further away from her North Country home.

At last, worn out by weariness and nervous strain, Ella
slept, too, and dreamt she was lost among the slag-heaps.
They were tipping, and she was right in the way of a loaded
truck. In another minute she'd be covered over with the
load of hot dross. She'd be beneath a smoking, fiery
avalanche!. . . A voice said in her ear: 'We're just coming
into King's Cross, dear. Wake up!. . . The poor child's
quite exhausted!'

Ella jumped up, rubbing the sleep from her eyes.

'King's Cross? That was the name of the station where

me Mam said I was to get out.'

'Yes, dear, London at last! What a night! I haven't slept a wink! . . . Oh, *thank* you' (to the young soldier), 'I'm afraid I don't know your name. So kind! I must really see this little girl to the end of her journey. Is this all your luggage, dear? Just the one case? It *is* a nice one, isn't it?'

'Miss Weston giv' it to us,' said Ella. 'She thought I mightn't have a one, and she was right. I didna.'

'Miss Weston *must* be a kind lady,' said her companion.

Ella fixed her great dark eyes on the speaker's face.

'Miss Weston ain't no lady,' she said. 'She's a dancer. She's the most wonderful dancer there has ever been. I seed her on television, and it's her as giv' us the scholarship to Sadler's Wells.'

'You don't mean to say you're *really* going to Sadler's Wells?' said the talkative lady. 'Come now – you're joking, aren't you? You're making it up!'

'No, I ain't, miss,' Ella said indignantly. 'What for should I make it up? And what for else should I be coming to London?'

'Well, I was wondering that, myself,' said the lady. 'I must say it seems odd, but of course if you *say* you're going to Sadler's Wells, I suppose you are. . . Come along, we'd better get a taxi.'

She was kind and meant well. She really wanted to help the forlorn child, but over and above this praiseworthy instinct was that of curiosity. She wanted to see where the child was going. She'd read the Sunday papers, and she'd watched and listened to all the television and radio thrillers. She knew all about the white slave traffic! All about the girls who disappeared! Who knew where this little girl might be going to? It was her plain duty . . .

The taxi sped along the almost deserted streets – London streets are never *quite* deserted, even at six-thirty in the morning. The talkative lady had asked Ella for the address of this Lady Bailey, and Ella had shown it to her, written on the back of an old envelope – number 42 Carsbroke Place, London, W.1.

'The West End!' said Ella's companion, with raised eyebrows. 'Well, I suppose there is as much vice in the West End as anywhere else – perhaps more!'

The streets got bigger and wider. They crossed Oxford Circus, and bowled down Regent Street. They turned off to the right and were suddenly in a wide square with gardens in the middle and Victorian porticoed mansions all round the sides.

'My goodness!' said the talkative lady to herself. 'How frightfully posh!'

The taxi stopped outside one of the tall houses, and the driver opened the door without getting out.

'Number 42,' he said. 'That right, lidy? Wot you said?'

The talkative lady gave him the fare and they got out. Taking her courage in both hands, Ella's companion mounted the marble steps, and behind her came Ella with her case, looking smaller than ever under the massive stone portico.

'We'd better ring the bell, hadn't we?' said the lady nervously. 'No – wait a minute! Perhaps you'd better go down there, dear' – she nodded towards a flight of steps leading down to the area – 'and ring that one. I'll stay here.' She still had at the back of her mind that Ella was going out to service.

'Yes, miss,' said Ella obediently. Whereupon she descended the steps and rang the bell. A pert maid with her cap on one side opened the door.

'Yes? What do you want? If you're selling anythink, we don't want nothink.'

'I – me name's Ella Sordy,' faltered the child.

'Well, why didn't you say so afore?' said the girl, who

113

was clearly not in a very good temper. 'Can't you read?' She pointed to a notice on the area railings. 'This is the trade entrance. Go up there and ring the bell.' She nodded towards the flight of steps down which Ella had just come, and slammed the area door.

'Oh!' said Ella's companion, who had, of course, been listening. 'Then I suppose it must be all right.' She pressed the bell rather timidly.

The massive door opened, as if the person inside had been standing on the mat, and Ella and the talkative lady found themselves staring up at a very dignified butler. His features betrayed no surprise at all. Little girls dressed in the cheapest and nastiest of mass-produced cotton dresses, accompanied by their mothers (for such he took Ella's companion to be), might stand on the steps of his London mansion every day of his life! Or perhaps he was expecting her.

'Good morning?' he said, with a question in his voice.

'Me name's Ella,' said the child.

'Yes, Ella Sordy,' put in the talkative lady, who had, by this time, discovered Ella's second name. 'She's just come off the night train, and she must be rightdown tired, poor little thing! This is the right address, I suppose. Number 42 Carsbroke Place?'

'That's right, madam,' said the man. 'Her ladyship is expecting Miss Sordy. Come in, miss.' He took her smart little case and, with a look, dismissed her companion. Obviously he had been told not to encourage mothers!

'Goodbye, dear!' called the talkative lady, who, by this time, had grown quite fond of Ella. 'And be good!' It was only after the door had shut behind Ella that she remembered her fears about the white slave traffic. She took her shopping-list out of her handbag and wrote number 42 Carsbroke Place upon it. She would call at the nearest police station and give the police the tip!

Chapter 2

Lady Bailey

The butler led the way into a high panelled room at the back of the house, through it, and into a small cloakroom fitted with a wash basin and a large mirror. There were clean towels on a heated chromium rail along one wall.

'You would like to have a wash, miss, I expect,' said the man, 'after your long journey? Your breakfast will be served immediately in the dining-room.' He nodded towards the room they had just left. 'Miss Patience – the young lady whose room you share – is not down yet.'

Left alone, Ella stared at the towels in awestruck amazement. There seemed to be dozens of them – six, anyway – and they were made of deep rose-pink linen with an embroidered monogram upon the corner of each. Which one ought she to use? It seemed a crying shame to soil any of them! Finally she washed cautiously in the snowy basin with a large tablet of scented soap, and dried herself on her hankie!

'Oh, Mam! Mam!' she said in her heart. 'What sorta place have I gotten to? I wish I was home, I do! I dinna want no breakfast!' The pangs of homesickness had effectively stifled the pangs of hunger. All Ella wanted at that moment was to escape from the snowy marble and glittering chromium of that super-cloakroom; to get away from that softly carpeted, panelled, spacious London house. Most of all to get out of range of the supercilious gaze of that dignified butler. But it was no use wishing. Here she was, and here she would have to stay. For one thing, how did one find one's way out, and, if one did, how could one open that monumental door without anyone hearing? Besides, her case – the treasured suitcase that Veronica Weston had given her – had vanished. She certainly wasn't going home without it! Last, but by no means the least important reason for staying, was that here she was going to learn to dance. It was this or nothing! Ella would go through more than this for the sake of her beloved dancing!

She plucked up her courage and crept back into the dining-room. Here the pert maid (whose bad temper was no doubt due to the fact that it was so early in the morning) served her with a bowl of cereal and cream, a fried egg, and a pot of milky coffee. Besides all this, there was toast, butter, and marmalade, and a bowl of fresh fruit. Ella had never eaten a breakfast like it in her life. Her meal at home was a slice of bread and marge, with a scrape of jam and a cup of weak tea. The tragedy was that she wasn't hungry, and so couldn't do justice to it. After a mouthful of cornflakes, she pushed them aside, and only out of sheer politeness did she tackle the egg. It stuck in her throat, and when she tried to wash it down with the coffee, she nearly choked. The pert maid patted her on the back obligingly. She was good-hearted, though pert, and her temper was improving as the day wore on. Besides, as she told the cook afterwards, she felt sorry for the plain-looking little thing. 'Miserable ain't the word!'

'If you've finished your breakfast,' she said, when Ella's face had returned to its normal pallor after the choking fit, 'I'll take you up to see Her Ladyship. Don't be frightened,' she added, 'she won't bite! She's awful kind.' She led the way back to the hall, and up a flight of wide stairs, so thickly carpeted that your footsteps made no sound, and you felt as if you were walking on deep moss, thought Ella. At the top of the staircase was a gallery, and round three sides of it were closed bedroom doors. The maid knocked on the nearest one.

'Come in!' said a voice.

Ella had never in her life seen a bedroom like this. At home her mam and dad slept in a square box-like room, with one small, oblong window looking out directly over the back yard, and indirectly over number 112 and 114's back yards. If you opened the window and put your head out, you could smell Willie Sprott's guinea-pigs at number 115 up the street!

The chief article of furniture in Mr and Mrs Sordy's bedroom was, as also in Lady Bailey's, a bed. But here the similarity ended. Me Mam and Me Dad's bed was made of black iron, with round knobs at top and bottom corners for decoration, and a mattress that sagged in the middle and creaked when you lay down on it. There were two threadbare blankets on the bed, and an ancient quilt. To do Me Mam justice, all these things – as well as the old lace curtains at the window – were quite clean. The floor was covered with cheap canvas, the pattern of which was entirely worn off by thirty-odd years of feet treading upon it. In fact, you could only see what colour it had once been in the corners and under the bed, where it hadn't been walked upon. A mat covered a large hole in front of the fireplace. The only other articles of furniture were a couple of bedroom chairs with the seats out, and a painted wash-stand upon which stood an old-fashioned jug and basin. A shallow alcove by the side of the fireplace was fitted with hooks and a curtain, and did duty for a wardrobe.

To get back to Lady Bailey's bedroom, on the threshold of which Ella stood. The immense floor – or so it seemed to Ella – was covered right up to the skirting-board with a leaf-green carpet, and the walls were shimmering cream and gold. The ceiling was like Heaven itself, so thick was it with fat cupids leaning on clouds. The bed was a splendid four-poster with brocaded hangings, and in it reclined a

117

large lady in an extremely low-cut nightdress. So fascinated was Ella by the lady's generous curves and by the ribbons and laces that rose and fell on her ample bosom, that she just stood there, saying nothing, whilst the maid closed the door softly on the two of them.

'Come over here, dear,' said the lady in the bed. 'I can't see you. I'm a little short-sighted.'

Ella advanced obediently over the mossy carpet, and stood waiting.

'So you're Ella?' said Lady Bailey. 'Recommended to me by my dear Veronica. I have great hopes of you, Ella. A dancer like Miss Weston wouldn't make a mistake in you. If she says you're good, then you must be.'

'Yes, miss,' said Ella. Then, remembering Ruth Fisher's orders not to call everyone 'miss', she hastily added: 'I mean, mam.'

'You can call me Lady Bailey, dear,' said the figure in the bed, taking a sip from a glass of orange-juice that stood on a small table near by. 'Well, I hope you'll be happy here, Ella.'

'I hope so, too, I'm sure, miss – I mean, mam – I mean Lady Bailey,' faltered poor Ella. 'I haven't never been nowhere like this afore.'

Inwardly Lady Bailey was a little dismayed, but, being essentially kind-hearted, she managed to hide her feelings.

'I do everything I can to make the dancers who come to live with me happy,' she told Ella. 'All I live for is to further their careers.'

'Yes, Lady Bailey,' said Ella. As time went on she found that what Lady Bailey said was quite true. This rich old woman had fallen in love with the ballet, and now her life centred round it. At first she had haunted the Wells, but this famous school does not – quite rightly – welcome visitors at its ballet classes, and, after a while, it had dawned upon her that she was being more than a bit of a nuisance.

So she had the brilliant idea of turning her big London house into a home for dancers. Some of these girls were the daughters of friends of hers; others were girls who had come from abroad and had nowhere to live. Actually Ella was the only really poor one among them. Lady Bailey had never housed a child who couldn't speak correct English, and who called her 'miss'! But her dear friend, Veronica, had asked her to take in the child, and she would do anything for Veronica. She found, later on, that although Ella's grammar was non-existent, and she obviously didn't know which knife and fork to use at table, yet she possessed fundamental good manners. She was kind and thoughtful, never pushed herself forward, and always offered elder people her seat in tubes and buses, no matter how tired she was herself.

'You can go now,' Lady Bailey said to her new protégée. 'I only wanted to see you and welcome you. Jenny will show you your room.' She rang a bell at her bedside, and the pert maid reappeared and conducted Ella round the gallery to a door at the far end. She knocked, whereupon the door opened, and a girl in a pale blue quilted satin dressing-gown appeared.

'Miss Patience – here's your new room-mate,' said the pert maid. She winked behind Ella's unconscious head, put Ella's small case inside the door, and fled, leaving the owner of the room staring in surprise at the newcomer. She'd certainly never expected a room-mate like this! A child in a cheap cotton dress that didn't hang properly, and strong black shoes.

'Oh – er – come in,' she said. 'You're Ella Sordy, aren't you?'

'Yes, miss,' said Ella.

'Oh, for goodness sake – my name is Patience – Patience Eliot!' exclaimed the girl. 'How old are you?'

'I'm going on fourteen,' said Ella.

'You look younger than that. I'm sixteen, and I'm in the Senior School. You'll be in the Junior?'

Ella nodded. She couldn't take her eyes off Patience Eliot. Never had she seen anyone quite so beautiful – anyone with so fine a skin, with hair so fair that it had a silvery sheen in the light, such big, velvety dark eyes. It didn't occur to her that her own eyes were just as beautiful.

Besides being beautiful, Patience was also kind-hearted. She cleared her silver toilet fittings to one side of the dressing-table and moved her clothes, hanging in the big wardrobe, so as to make room for the newcomer's.

'There!' she said. 'Now you can unpack. Where's your trunk?'

'I ain't got no trunk,' said Ella. 'I've only gotten me case that Miss Weston give us.'

'You really mean that Veronica Weston gave you that lovely case?' said Patience, in such awestruck tones that Ella stared at her, amazed.

'Yes, miss – Patience, I mean.'

'And it was she who sent you here?'

'Yes.'

'Then you *must* be good,' declared Patience. 'I'm just longing to see you dance, Ella.'

The magic word 'dance' revived Ella.

'Is there anywhere where you can dance in this house?' she asked.

'I should just say there is! Wait till I show you!' exclaimed Patience. 'Lady Bailey has had the whole top floor – where the attics used to be – made into a studio. It's *huge*, with mirrors galore, and lots of *barres*.'

'Oo, miss – I mean Patience!' said Ella.

'Most of us are too tired – or too lazy – after our work at school ever to practise there,' went on Patience. 'Much to Lady Bailey's disgust! I believe the poor darling really *likes* to watch us practise!'

Ella stared at Patience with wondering dark eyes. Fancy calling Lady Bailey 'poor darling'!

'Well, now let me help you to unpack your case,' said Patience helpfully. 'I have a few minutes before breakfast, and it won't take long, if that's all you've got!' She seized the blue case and snapped open the clasps.

'Oh, no, miss – if you don't mind. I'd rather do it mesel',' said Ella, laying hands on her case firmly. Suddenly she felt she didn't want this lovely girl in the satin dressing-gown to see her shabby underclothes. To be true, Miss Weston had sent Me Mam a generous cheque, together with a letter telling her to 'fit Ella out for the Wells', but Me Mam had taken most of it to pay off the arrears on the television set, and there had only been enough left to buy the cheap frock and the shoes. So Ella's smart case was filled with the jumble sale vests, pants and nighties that composed her usual wardrobe.

'OK,' said Patience cheerfully. 'There goes the gong! You can do it while we're having breakfast. You've had yours, I expect?'

Ella nodded and, when Patience had gone, she set about hanging up her made-over skirts in the wardrobe next to Patience's fine pleated ones, and her washed-out print frocks next to the pastel linen dresses of her room-mate. (Fortunately there were plenty of vacant hangers. Ella had never owned a hanger!) After this, she laid her underwear in one of the drawers Patience had indicated, and then straightened herself. Her unpacking was done!

Chapter 3

Ella at the Wells

'This is the Wells, Ella!' said Patience next morning. Although she, herself, didn't start the day until an hour later, she had made herself responsible for the younger girl. 'See the historic name on the door – 45 Colet Gardens. Sadler's Wells School. Cross yourself, or mutter a prayer, or something! It's very sacred, I assure you! . . . Oh, no – *we* ordinary students don't go in there. Only visitors, governors, royalty, Madame herself, enter beneath the sacred portal! We go in *here*.' She led the way into a sort of conservatory. 'This is the Winter Garden. Nice, isn't it? . . . Your cloakrooms are over there to the left. The students' dressing-rooms are down there.' She indicated a short flight of stone steps.

The school was full of activity, although it was so early in the morning. There were girls everywhere – and quite a lot of boys, too. Girls dashing about in tights and tunics; girls standing looking at the noticeboards; girls sitting on the tables; yet more smaller girls in the same school uniform that Ella wore, staring at her curiously. Thank goodness, her uniform was right, anyway, she thought! She'd found it waiting for her at Carsbroke Place when she arrived, together with several pairs of ballet shoes, two pairs of black tights, and one pink pair. Also a garment like an abbreviated cardigan. Patience had explained that it was a 'cross-over' – to wear when it was cold.

'They don't restrict or hide the movements,' she added, 'so we're allowed to wear them. This is your hair-band and your belt. You have a different coloured belt according to the part of the school you're in.'

So Ella didn't feel quite such a fish out of water as she had done when she had arrived at Carsbroke Place. At all events, she *looked* just like everyone else, and this, as everyone knows, is all-important to a schoolgirl. But as for the rest, she found that the Wells wasn't the least bit like her old school at Blackheath. For one thing, the classes were small – just about a dozen pupils in each. It hardly seemed like school at all to Ella, used to fifty or sixty! For another, you didn't chant 'po-try' or 'tables' in unison, and you were encouraged to ask questions in a way that would have been called 'cheeky' at her old school. When you spoke to the mistresses (they weren't called 'teachers' here), you stood up to do it, and you called them by their names, not just 'miss' . . . 'Yes, Miss Callendar,' you said. In fact, you stood up whenever you were spoken to. They were ever so polite, thought Ella. Why they even curtsied at the end of the ballet class, and nobody laughed!

And what a ballet class! Ella had never imagined anything like it. There were real *barres*, instead of chairs, to put your hand on. And mirrors! Why, there were mirrors everywhere! There was a gallery up above, too, and a low stage called a 'rostrum'. Ella discovered that the big room was called the Baylis Hall. Before she went home that evening, she crept back through the square entrance-hall, up the stairs, and stood on the threshold of the room. Lots and lots of famous people had practised at these very *barres*, she thought – people like Veronica Weston. And now here she was, Ella Sordy, doing the same thing! She crept forward and smoothed the nearest *barre* gently with her hand. Here had Veronica's hand rested!

'Well? Do you think you'll be able to put up with it?' said a voice behind her.

Ella jumped guiltily, and the colour flooded to her face.

123

She hadn't seen the man standing there in the shadow.

'Oh, I'm sorry – I didn't know—'

'It's all right – don't look so frightened. You weren't doing anything wrong. I just wondered what you were thinking?'

'I was thinking of Veronica Weston,' Ella said simply. 'She must have done them *pliés* on this very *barre* – the same as wot I 'ave!'

'So she must,' said the man. 'How original of you to think of it! I've often wondered, myself, if any of the students here think of the ones who have gone before, and now it seems *you* have. What is your name?'

'Me name's Ella – Ella Sordy.'

'Well, Ella Sordy, you've begun well,' said the slightly sarcastic voice. 'You've begun by *thinking* – which is a thing some people make a point of never doing. Not in my classes, anyway!. . . Yes' (as Ella fixed her large, dark eyes upon him) 'I'm a dancing instructor. Name Delahaye. We shall meet by and by. I expect you'll be told I'm a tartar! Don't believe *all* you hear. Goodbye, Ella – and do go on thinking. It's very refreshing!'

He vanished, and Ella looked after him in wonderment.

'He was havin' us on!' she said to herself. 'He was havin' a bit of a joke!'

As a matter of fact, Mr Gilbert Delahaye's manner was deceptive. He said sarcastic things and acted the temperamental ballet master, but this was merely a pose. Actually he was a very simple, kind-hearted person, and merely used his sarcastic tongue to spur his pupils on. But this Ella did not find out for some time. She was very frightened of him at first. He shouted – oh, not at her. She was far too careful to keep well away from him! He banged with his stick! He scowled! He raged! One day he stood at the top of the room watching with feigned boredom the frantic scuffle that went on to obtain a place in the front of his class. The same girls always got there. Angela, fair, with a squashed pug-dog face (his mental description of her!), and hard blue eyes. A temperamental blonde, called Diane. Two sisters, Phyllis and Marion, who had been there longer than anyone else, and so took front places by right. A girl called Daphne. Gilbert Delahaye disliked them all. Yes, the whole pushing, shoving row! The one he *really* wanted to see – where was she, now? Ah, yes – in the back row, as usual!

He banged on the floor with his stick, and waited for silence.

'When you have all quite finished pushing and shoving,' he remarked, 'we will do a little change round. The front row will change places with the back. Yes, you – Angela, Diane, Phyllis, Marion, Daphne – at the back, please! Oh, I know it is incredible, but I have really become quite tired of looking at your well-known faces! For a change we will have in front Mary, Katherine, Yvonne, Sally, and – what is your name? Yes, the girl at the back?'

'Ella,' said the child, her heart thumping. This terrible man was going to bait her! 'Ella Sordy.'

'Ah, yes, of course – Ella. We have met before, have we not? Forgive me for not remembering the name, but really, I so very seldom catch a glimpse of you, it's not to be wondered at, is it? Yes, Ella Sordy – in the middle of the front row, if you please. Now, we will begin!'

The class progressed and, out of the corner of his eye – even when he was addressing other members of the class, Mr Delahaye watched Ella, just as Mary Martin had done. She was beautiful; she was expressive; her movements were a delight to the eye. But, oh, so meek! So maddeningly, indescribably meek! Something must be done about it, or she'd never get anywhere. She'd be lost! He dismissed the class, but kept back Ella Sordy with a peremptory wave of his stick.

'Ella Sordy – one moment, if you please,'

Ella was so frightened that she went back to her Blackheath form of address – a thing she hadn't done for a long time.

'Yes, miss,' she said trembling.

For a second or two Gilbert Delahaye stood looking at her. Then the storm broke.

'Do I look like a "miss"?' he raged. 'Do I? My dear, good child, are you suffering from an inferiority complex, or what is the matter with you?'

Ella didn't know what he meant, but it was obviously something bad, so she whispered: 'N-no, please, Mr Delahaye.'

'Well, *I-say-yes!*' said Mr Delahaye, accenting the words with his stick. 'It must stop, do you hear? You dance well – extremely well. You look beautiful, yet, when you speak, you tremble and say "Yes, miss" like a trapped mouse! I won't have it, understand?'

'Yes, miss,' said poor Ella. 'I mean, no, Mr Delahaye.'

'For goodness sake,' raged the exasperated ballet master, '*do* something, Ella! Don't just stand there like a piece of wet tripe, and say "Yes, miss"! Stamp your feet! Burst into tears! Throw something at me, if you like! Anything, *anything* rather than *"Yes, miss"!*' The vicious imitation of his tone of voice was too much for Ella. She did what he said, and burst into tears.

Immediately Mr Delahaye was all contrition.

'Look – I didn't mean that really.' He put a kind hand on her shoulder. 'I was just infuriated beyond words' (if he had stopped to think, he would have seen the humour in this statement!) 'that you should be so confoundedly meek – you who have the makings of a great dancer – while some of the others, students who will never do anything at all, push in front of you. Don't cry, Ella! Can't you tell me what is the matter?'

'It's me voice!' sobbed Ella. 'It's the way I talks. They none of them talks like what I do. They imitate us!'

'They do, do they?' said Mr Delahaye dangerously. 'Let me catch them at it! Just let me catch them!'

'If I could talk like Angela—'

'Don't you *dare!*' broke in Mr Delahaye. 'Don't you *dare* to copy that shrill, affected, little minx! If I had to listen to Angela Dykes talking for more than a couple of hours a week, I should go stark, staring, raving mad! Your voice, Ella, is at least sweet and low, even if your grammar is faulty, and you're apt to say "Yes, miss" at the wrong moments! But I see your point. Well, if you *must* copy somebody, why don't you take Patience Eliot for your model? She lives where you do, doesn't she, and she's at least got a *pleasing* voice, and her grammar is impeccable.'

Ella didn't know the meaning of impeccable, but she was rapidly losing her fear of Mr Delahaye.

'Yes, Mr Delahaye,' she said. 'I'll try. Patience Eliot is me room-mate.'

He said nothing more for a moment, merely remained leaning against one of the *barres*, apparently deep in thought. Finally he straightened himself.

'Ever go to the theatre, Ella?' he asked, digging into one of his pockets. 'Apart from the ballet, I mean?'

'No, Mr Delahaye,' said Ella. She didn't add: 'I haven't got no money,' but he guessed it.

'Well, here are two tickets – one for you, and one for your friend. You've got a friend, haven't you?'

Ella shook her head.

'Then find one quickly. Life isn't life without a friend! What about that room-mate of yours – Patience Eliot? She seems a nice girl. Why not ask her to go with you?'

'Oh, miss – I mean, Mr Delahaye, I wouldn't dare!'

'Dare! Dare! . . .' The temperamental ballet master began. Then, seeing the consternation on the girl's face, he laughed and added: 'You try it, and see. Your luck may be in! By the way, it's Spanish dancing, this time. It does you good to see other forms of the art you're studying upon occasions – stops you getting narrow-minded. See what you think of Rosita and Angelo at the New Theatre. And by the way, when I said copy Patience Eliot, I meant her *voice*. Nothing else, please. I prefer *your* dancing!'

'Thank you, Mr Delahaye,' said Ella, and she gave him one of her rare smiles.

Chapter 4

Fairy Godmother

The term went by and, though Ella didn't realize it herself, she changed considerably. For one thing, she had followed Gilbert Delahaye's advice, and asked Patience Eliot to go with her to see Rosita and Angelo. Moreover Patience had accepted. Ella had become quite friendly with Patience after that, though she still pulled the pale blue curtains, dividing her cubicle from her room-mate's, closely round her when she went to bed at night, but this wasn't because she didn't love Patience dearly, but because she was ashamed of her shrunken, felted underclothing. Patience's underclothes were beautiful. Ella knew this because Patience wasn't at all shy about showing them off. The things she wore underneath were as lovely as those she wore on top, thought Ella wonderingly. Pale pink, and blue, and white satin and nylon garments, trimmed with lace and embroidery, and she had a black chiffon nightie! It looked lovely with her fair hair. Ella longed and longed for a nightgown like that!

Ella had stopped saying 'Give us a one' and 'I haven't got no' whatever it happened to be. She had learned not to address everyone as 'miss', and now said 'Mr Delahaye' and 'Miss Callendar' and 'Lady Bailey' even without thinking! She had ceased to find the Sadler's Wells School strange, though at first it might have been the Zoo, so different was it from her old school! At the latter the accent was all on 'numbers' and 'reading' and 'writing'. Here, they weren't nearly so particular about arithmetic or spelling (though, of course, you learnt these things, too) as they were about things called 'appreciation of music' and 'art' and 'essays'. Ella went to the Albert Hall with her schoolmates and listened, spellbound, to well-known symphony orchestras conducted by famous men. She walked round the Tate Gallery and stood lost in a trance of sheer delight before the paintings of Old Masters, until somebody nudged her and said: *'Ella!* Are you coming? Miss Callendar's gone already!' She looked at modern paintings, and spent hours in libraries, looking at colour-prints of paintings that were not to be found in the English galleries. The 'Madonna of the Rocks', by Leonardo da Vinci, was one of her favourites. 'She's so young and lovely,' Ella whispered to Patience. (Note that she no longer said 'luver-ly'.) The two of them went to Battersea Park, looked at the sculpture, and didn't like it much.

'They all look like *something,* but I don't know what,' said Ella, which was, perhaps, exactly what the sculptor wanted them to think!

Ella's appearance had changed, too. She had grown a little taller and slimmer in the body, but her peaked face had filled out, and she had now a lovely complexion – still pale, but with the faintest tinge of pink, like one drop of cochineal dropped into a bowl of cream. This was due, no doubt, to the exercise and good food, for Lady Bailey saw that 'her girls', as she called them, had 'proper meals'. No bread and jam and cups of tea, or fried fish and chips drowned in vinegar were forthcoming at Carsbroke Place! So the dimples had crept into Ella's cheeks, and her hair now gleamed with life, so that it was no longer raven black, but had blue lights in it, due to much brushing by the pert maid who could be quite friendly when you got on her right side.

After Mr Delahaye's outburst, when he had presented the tickets to her, her behaviour had changed, too – in his class, anyway, although in the others she still stayed shrinking at the back. But in Mr Delahaye's class she remained in the front row. She didn't do this by pushing, but simply by refusing to be pushed. One might call it passive resistance! As quick as lightning she was up in the front row, and in the front row she remained, push who might! Her adored Mr Delahaye had told her to stay there, so she stayed.

It was only a few days to the end of term and everyone was in the lounge talking about the holidays. Ella wasn't to go home. That had been clearly understood from the beginning. No holidays at Pit Street! Although Miss Weston and Miss Martin hadn't said so to Ella, they had discussed it between themselves, and had decided that the less Ella saw of Pit Street, Me Mam, Lily, and D'reen, the better!

'But won't you be awfully lonely?' said Patience one morning. She had just got a letter from home, and was reading parts of it out aloud.

'Yes – it must be nice to have people of your own to go home to,' said Ella wistfully. She knew now, of course, that Me Mam, Lily, and D'reen, were no kin to her.

Patience's lovely face clouded.

'As a matter of fact, I haven't many people belonging to me, either,' she confessed. 'My mother – she's in Paris, you know, or somewhere abroad. I never see her. She and my father don't live together any more. My father spends most of his time here in London.'

'In London?' echoed Ella. 'Why, then you can see him any time you want to.'

'Y-es.' Patience sounded doubtful, and it was obvious to Ella that the relationship between Colonel Eliot and his daughter was not a very close one. 'I – I don't think that my father is so terribly interested in me as to want to see me very often. It's really rather amazing that he let me come here to study ballet. I haven't yet got over the shock!

I think, myself, that it must be due to Lady Bailey. She's a great friend of my father's, you know. So you see, Ella, I'm nearly as much an orphan as you! Of course there's David – he's my half-brother. I *adore* him! Oh, and by the way, David is to be an usher at Jane's wedding.' (Ella had, of course, heard all about Jane Foster's forthcoming marriage to Guy Charlton, who was Patience's cousin, and how Jane had given up her ballet career.) 'I'm to be a bridesmaid. The other two are Mariella – she's Jane's cousin, you know – and Elizabeth Lister. She's a great friend of mine. Her brother, Richard, is to be another usher. He's up at Cambridge, but of course the wedding's in the vacation – 26th of December, just after Christmas, and Jane is to wear white velvet. Oh, you should see the bridesmaids' dresses. They're velvet too, only in palest blue, and we carry bouquets of white jasmine and stephanotis. That's the sort with the heavenly smell! There are to be two smaller bridesmaids – about as big as you, only as a matter of fact they're years younger! You're so small for your age. Their names are Margaret Mainwaring (she's usually called Meg) and Gillian Shafto. They're wearing white velvet, like the bride, only of course made in a younger style.'

Ella sighed. It sounded so lovely. She wished she could be there!

Patience looked up from her letter, conscience-stricken.

'Oh, I'm *so* sorry!' she apologized. 'Here am I rambling on about my holiday when you aren't going home at all. If only—'

'If only what?'

'Oh, nothing,' Patience said. After all, she couldn't explain to Ella (even if she wanted to) that, had her appearance been different, she would have invited her to Dewburn for the Christmas holiday. But she pictured Ella at Dewburn among her friends (especially at a smart wedding!) and knew that it wouldn't be kind to ask Ella there – Ella in her uneven, made-over skirts, and old jumpers that didn't fit her anywhere. No, far better to leave her here at the Wells, where nobody set much store on appearances – except in the ballet classes, and Ella's ballet things were beautiful. Veronica Weston had seen to that! As a matter of fact, Ella's everyday clothes were clean and neat certainly, but what could one do with a skirt that had belonged to Mrs Jobson, who had a forty-inch waist, and had been bought at the jumble sale for ten pence. No wonder Patience sighed, for she was very fond of Ella and would dearly have loved to take her home with her.

'There are to be four ushers altogether,' she went on, turning back to the letter. 'That awful Nigel Monkhouse I told you about is to be one. Of course, he's Jane's cousin, so they couldn't leave him out! The fourth is someone called Timothy Roebottom. I don't know him myself, but Elizabeth says he's one of Richard's friends. His father is a vicar somewhere, and he's up at Cambridge with Richard – Timothy is, I mean. Richard's father is Vicar of Dewburn, you know – our village, but I expect I've told you.'

If she had been less engrossed in her letter she would have seen a flood of pink spread over Ella's meadowsweet pale face. Timothy Roebottom! It seemed years and years ago since he had befriended her! Her thoughts flew back to Blackheath . . . the Sunday School . . . Timothy's ancient car . . . the grey and white ballet dress. How she wished she could have been at this wedding with Patience! All this time she had kept the image of her prince charming in her heart, though she had never seen him from that day to this.

But just at this moment something happened that drove even Timothy Roebottom from Ella's thoughts. The pert maid put her head round the door, fixed her eyes on Ella, and announced: 'There's a lady to see you, Miss Ella. She's in the sitting-room.'

'A lady? To see me?' exclaimed Ella. 'Oh, I think you must be mistaken, Jenny. It must be someone else she wants to see.'

'No, miss – she said "Miss Ella Sordy", quite plain,' insisted the maid. 'It's a Mrs Scott, but she said you would know her better if I said Miss Weston.'

'Veronica Weston!' said a chorus of awestricken voices. 'Oh, Ella – you *are* lucky!' By their envious glances it seemed that even Ella Sordy had something other people would give their eyes for! As for Ella, herself, her face lit up with excitement. If a warm place in her heart was kept for the image of her prince, a fairy godmother occupied the throne! She ran down the wide, shallow staircase and was on the threshold of the sitting-room before you could wink an eyelash, as Mary, one of the students, put it.

Veronica looked at Ella and saw that her experiment was proving a success. Never had she beheld such a change in a girl. She had improved beyond recognition. On the other hand, what on earth had the child done with her clothes – got them on back to front or what? Or perhaps her dress sense was undeveloped as yet!

'Well, Ella,' she said, 'I needn't ask you how you are, for I hardly knew you! You're a different girl! Why, you look positively blooming! But, my dear – whatever have you got on? Is this' – she touched the skirt Ella was wearing – 'the best your mother could do with the money I sent her? Where on earth did she buy it?'

'At – at the jumble sale,' faltered Ella.

'The *jumble sale?*' repeated Veronica in astonishment. 'But what on earth possessed your mother to go there? What did she do with the cheque I sent her?'

'It wasn't really Mam's fault,' said Ella. 'You see, Miss Weston, the man came about the television set and there was such a lot of instalments due, and if Mam hadn't—'

'Ah, *now* I understand!' exclaimed Veronica. 'You needn't go on, Ella. I suppose you got *no* new clothes at all?'

'Oh, yes, I did,' said Ella, striving to be fair to her Mam. 'I got an art silk dress at Murreys, but when it was washed it ran – I mean, the colours did.'

Veronica's thoughts went back to her own childhood, to the day when her cousin Fiona, in a fit of jealousy, had thrown Veronica's cheap print frock into the bath and the colours had run, in like manner. She felt again the agony of that moment and her heart burned for Ella.

'So then you had nothing to wear but these horrors?' she said. 'I might have known! I blame myself very much, Ella. I should have seen to it personally. You see – it was my baby coming just then—'

'Oh, yes,' broke in Ella. 'Your little baby! How is she, Miss Weston?'

'She's very well indeed,' said Veronica, her dark eyes glowing at the mention of her darling. 'You must see her very soon, Ella. But now we must do something about your clothes – now, this very minute. Go and ask Grayson to call me a taxi. You're coming with me to Harridges!'

Never had Clotilde, the French buyer in the teenage department of Harridges great store, had such a thrilling afternoon! First of all, for the world-famous ballerina, Veronica Weston, to walk into her department and demand her personal attention! *Oh, là, là!* Then for the ballerina to demand a complete trousseau – and how you say eet? outfeet – for *la petite,* the leetle girl she has in tow – a most *bourgeois* leetle girl. *Non pas!* Not *bourgeois* exactly. You could not call her that. She walk beau-ti-fully, *par example,* like a princess! But her clothes – *mon Dieu!* (Clotilde threw up her hands in horror when recounting the incident to her friend, the buyer of the Furs, that evening.) *'Impossible à décrire, ma chère!* All one could say was that they fitted where they met, and they did not meet in many places! Enough to make laugh – or cry! *La pauvre gosse!* And now for the clothes – they must be of all kinds. First the underneaths, as one say in England. The *chemises* – camineeks; the sleeps (pardon, *je veux dire* "slips", *comme c'est difficile à dire!*). And then the skirts and jumps. All quite perfect – the skirts hanging *so,* and the jumps of the finest cashmere. Nossing is ask the price of! Nossing is too good! . . . then we must 'ave *des robes.* Frocks – *une, deux, trois!* Also a frock for *les grandes occasions* – ze partee! *Enfin,* a soot – a skirt and a coat to match such as ze Eengleesh adore! Flannel, *gris* like ze Eengleesh sky! *Mademoiselle, la petite,* will wear 'im now. She put 'im on. *Et voilà!* All is transformed *dans un petit moment!* She 'as a form of ze most beau-ti-ful (*c'est entendu – la petite est danseuse elle-même!*). Zey walk out of ze shop, and by now, ze news as run around zat ze great Veronica Weston is in my department, and all gather to look and admire. All of the most discreet, *naturellement! Oh, là, là!* Eet was, *en effet,* an afternoon of ze most entrancing!'

And now to get back to Ella. She and Veronica walked back to Carsbroke Place so as to give Ella's new costume an airing, as Veronica put it! As they passed a shop with a large full-length mirror in the window, Ella beheld a beautiful young lady, and by her side walked a smaller beautiful young lady – a slender girl, dressed in a perfectly fitting grey flannel suit, narrow black suède shoes, and the finest of silk stockings. This, mark you, was Ella Sordy of a short hour ago! Cinderella's fairy godmother in the fairy-story could not have effected a more startling transformation!

When she walked into the students' sitting-room there was a sudden silence. Then a gasp.

'*Ella!* We thought you were a stranger at first – a new student! . . . My! My! You sure do look beautiful!' (This from Susan, a Canadian student.) 'Where did you get those clothes?'

'Harridges,' said Ella.

'I must say you sure look like it!' drawled Susan. 'Yes, sir!'

Upstairs in her bedroom Ella opened her drawers and tumbled on to the floor all the jumble sale bargains acquired during the last ten years by Me Mam. Out they all came, and in went her new wardrobe – cotton, fine as gossamer; *crêpe de Chine*, shimmering like moonlight; satin, smooth as a baby's skin.

On her bed, ready for tonight, Ella laid out the prize of all – a black chiffon nightdress. Veronica had laughed when, in answer to her question: 'What sort of nighties would you like, Ella?' Ella had replied: 'I think they're all lovely, Miss Weston, but—'

'But what, Ella?'

'If you don't mind – I'd like a *black* one.'

'Black?' Veronica was startled. Lots of people wore black underclothes, of course, but she hadn't thought that Ella—

'You see,' explained Ella, 'Patience has one.'

'Oh, I *see!* Patience is very fair, isn't she?. . . Yes, I thought so. Well, don't expect, my dear, to look so ravishing in your black nightie as Patience Eliot does in hers! However, you may have it – it will be part of your education!'

And Ella found that it was true. The black chiffon nightie, lovely though it was, made her look sallow. She learnt a very valuable lesson from it – never to buy any article of dress merely because someone else looked nice in it! She gave the black nightie to Patience as a birthday present and wore, instead, the lovely pale pink one that made her look like a dewy rosebud, or the white that brought out the blue lights in her black hair.

Chapter 5

A Change of Plans

Oh, the delicious excitement of a wedding – especially when you're one of the bridesmaids! So thought Mariella, as she lifted her pale blue velvet bridesmaid's dress out of its box and hung it up in her wardrobe.

'Thrice a bridesmaid, never a bride!' she said aloud. 'This is only my second time, but I shall have to be careful in future!'

'I shouldn't worry, if I were you,' laughed Patience, who had come over from Dewburn to stay until the wedding was over. 'You're most awfully pretty, you know, Mariella. I think your hair is lovely! I don't think there's much chance of *you* being left on the shelf!'

'That's all very well for you,' answered Mariella. 'You're only a kid. Wait till you're my age – nineteen. In fact, I'm nearly twenty!'

'Most people think that twenty is very young to get married,' observed Patience.

'Oh, I wasn't actually thinking of getting *married*,' said Mariella. 'I was really meaning *engaged*.'

'Well, the one usually means the other, doesn't it?' laughed Patience. 'Personally, I'm not going to get married till I'm ever so old – twenty-four, at least. I'm going to dance first, and then like Jane, I shall stop right at the top of my career. Only I shan't do it quite so soon.'

'How will you manage to stay on your peak?' teased Mariella.

'Oh, I've got awfully good balance!' laughed Patience.

'Gilbert doesn't think so in his ballet class, but *I* know I have! I think it's a mistake to get married *too* young. All your fun stops, and you get lots of responsibilities. Look at Fiona! What on earth possessed her to get married at eighteen?'

'I expect Fiona wonders that now!' said Mariella wisely. 'I think she was afraid of being poor. Now she's bored with being rich! But I should like to know, Patience, where your fun, as you call it, comes in? From what I remember of ballet, it's nothing but work, work, work until you drop!'

'Oh, but I like it,' Patience assured her. 'I adore dancing! I do get some fun, too. *This*, for instance.' She held up a short tulle veil aganst her fair hair. 'How lovely this will look with my wreath of real jasmine!'

'Because tomorrow is Christmas Eve,' said Mariella, 'Jane and Guy are going to midnight mass together, and then church on Christmas morning. I think that's a lovely thing to do the day before one's wedding, don't you?'

'Yes, I do,' agreed Patience. 'It's just like Jane! Lots of people think so much about their dress, and the bridesmaids, and the presents, and the reception, that they forget all about the most important part – the religious side of the wedding. I'm afraid I'm a bit like that!'

Mariella laughed. Patience's big, dark eyes were so solemn you couldn't help it.

'Wait till your own wedding comes along!' she said.

'That's nearly eight years away – if I don't get married till I'm twenty-four,' said Patience. 'It seems a very long time, doesn't it? Perhaps I'll make it twenty-three! This wedding has made me want to marry someone quickly. Only it would have to be someone nice, like Guy!'

'Y-es,' said Mariella. Her thoughts had flown to Nigel. She hadn't seen much of him since their Edinburgh meeting at the end of the summer term. He'd shown her all too plainly that he was annoyed with her for climbing Arthur's

Seat with Robin Campbell. The fact that the mare Nigel had bought from Jock O'Dowd had proved to be a bad bargain hadn't helped matters. If Mariella hadn't gone off climbing with Robin, he wouldn't have been let in for that mare. So argued Nigel. He'd told her so, too! Oh, well, thought Mariella, Nigel was an usher at Jane's wedding, so she was bound to see him there, although, as chief bridesmaid, she'd actually be walking up the aisle with Robin, Guy's best man. She'd seen quite a lot of Robin lately. He'd asked her to several concerts, and she was going to the Daffodil Ball in Newcastle with him in March. That seemed a long time off, but, as Robin had said, the tickets got sold very quickly.

She was deep in her thoughts about Nigel when the bedroom door flew open and Jane appeared. It was obvious from her appearance that something was wrong.

'Oh, Mariella – Patience—' she gasped. 'The most awful thing has happened!'

'What has?' Mariella said tranquilly. She was used, by now, to Jane and her temperamental ways.

'Meg – the little bridesmaid – the one's who's to walk with Gillian – she's got measles!'

'Oh!' This really *was* serious. Both Mariella and Patience got up from their seat on Mariella's bed in consternation.

'How do you know?'

'She's just rung up – at least, her mother has – and she's all over spots. It's just too awful!'

'Yes, it is rather devastating,' agreed Patience. 'But we'll manage somehow. Gillian will just have to walk by herself.'

'Oh, but you don't understand, said Jane. 'She won't. That's the awful part of it. She only consented to be a bridesmaid on the condition that somebody else walked with her. She's frightfully shy, you know.'

'We all know!' said Mariella with feeling. She had suffered from the shyness of Gillian! 'Well, she'll just have

140

to put up with it, or else you'll have to manage with just Patience and me.'

'But that will *ruin* the procession,' declared Jane, almost in tears. Temperamental at any ordinary time, she was more 'on edge' than ever now, two days before her wedding! 'Besides,' she went on, 'there are the *dresses*. They're finished down to the last button and, oh, Mariella – they're so *beautiful!*'

'Well, we can't do anything about it, I'm afraid. Measles are measles—' began Mariella. But Patience broke in excitedly:

'Oh, but we *can!* I know someone who will walk with Gillian. She's just the right size, and she's a dancer, and she walks just beautifully! There'll be no nonsense about shyness with *her!*'

'Who is it?' said the others, both together.

'Her name's Ella,' said Patience. 'She's my room-mate at Carsbroke Place, and she's spending the holidays all by herself, so she'll be thrilled to bits to come up to the wedding. She knows all about it! I'll ring her up and she can get a sleeper, and be here in the morning . . . Wait – isn't Mariella's mother coming up tonight, too, Jane? . . . Well, then that's the very thing! They can travel together, and it won't be so lonely for Ella. She'll adore travelling with the famous ballerina, Irma Foster. Who wouldn't!'

So it happened that Ella travelled north on Christmas Eve in a first-class sleeper with Irma Foster, one of England's greatest dancers. For quite a long time she lay watching her coat joggling on its hanger from a hook on the wall. It was her new coat bought at Harridges a few days after the other things. Veronica and she had forgotten about a winter coat, so she had gone all by herself and chosen it. It was dark brown with a fur lining. It had a little fur collar and a cap to match. Not *real* fur, mind you – Ella was careful about that! She had not forgotten Gloria and the squirrel coat and, as she explained to the bewildered Clotilde, who had other views: 'I should hate to wear a darling leopard on my head!' But there was more to the coat than this – oh, much more! It was completely reversible. So that when you wanted to go to a 'partee', as Clotilde pronounced it, you turned it inside out, and *voilà!* You had a real fur coat. Well, anyway (with a shrug), one of fur fabric almost of the indistinguishable. *Très chic!*

On a shelf beside her bed lay Ella's lovely new under-clothes, neatly folded. Yes, she had a real bed, this time! No longer did tears trickle down her small nose. She was going to be bridesmaid at a wedding of a real ballerina! She was going to spend Christmas with her adored Patience! She was going to meet again her charming prince! She was completely and blissfully happy!

The train rushed on through the frosty moonlight and arrived at Newcastle at an unearthly hour in the morning. The occupants of the first-class sleepers, snuggled under their eiderdowns, determined not to venture out into the cold station until they had to! Irma Foster and little Ella Sordy were two of the last. A couple of porters hovered round them respectfully. Irma Foster commanded respect wherever she went. All her life people had waited on her and had rushed round to do things for her, so she took it as a matter of course. She waved in a lordly manner at her pigskin cases with their holland covers, and a few minutes later they were both in the big Dewburn car which had been sent to meet them.

'Now we *have* got all the luggage, haven't we?' she said, as they swung out of the station yard. 'The two cases of mine, and one of yours, and the square ballet case. By the way, what did you want that for?' She looked down at Ella inquiringly. The child wasn't pretty, but there was something fascinating about her. She would like to see her

142

dance. As if in answer to her thoughts, Ella answered:

'Patience said on the telephone would I please bring a ballet dress. They're having a ball on the night of the wedding, you know, and they thought people might like me to dance for them. Patience says she's been asked to dance, too. She said I had to be sure to ask permission from the Wells. They don't allow you to dance in public, you know, but I'm afraid I didn't have time to get in touch with nobody – I mean *any*body.'

'Well, *I* give you permission,' said Irma Foster. 'I have quite a lot to do with the Wells, you know.'

'Oh, thank you,' said Ella. 'That will be all right, then. I wonder if Miss Weston will be at the wedding? Patience said she was sure to be because she's a very great friend of Miss Foster – Jane Foster.'

'Oh, so you know Veronica?'

'Oh, yes,' said Ella, her large, dark eyes glowing. 'It was Miss Weston who sent us – I mean *me* – to the Wells. She gave me the scholarship.'

'Did she indeed?' said the ballerina, who was becoming more and more intrigued. 'Then you *must* be a beautiful dancer. I'm longing to see you!'

Chapter 6

Jane's Wedding

The day after Christmas – Jane's wedding-day – dawned cold and blue, with a bright sun and a sprinkling of snow.

'It's a typically Swiss day!' said Mariella to Patience, as they helped the bride to dress. 'Most unfair, Jane, when you're flying to Switzerland directly after the ceremony for the first part of your honeymoon!'

'I suppose the name of the place where you're going is a dead, dark secret?' said Patience.

'As dark as the inside of your hat!' laughed Jane. After being 'on edge' all the week, she was now as calm and unruffled as Crag Lough on a summer's day. As always, her knack of rising to the occasion had come to her aid. Her wedding was like a performance – a gala performance – and she must, and would, be at her best!

'I'll tell you two, though,' she added, 'provided you won't tell anyone else. We're going to Wengernalp to ski. Guy's an expert, and he's going to teach me. Wengernalp is a tiny place up above Wengen, and we're going to stay at a hotel perched all by itself 8,000 feet up, facing a great wall of mountains – the Mönch, the Eiger, the Jungfrau, the Silberhorn, and goodness knows what others! Oh, it will be lovely! We shall stay there a fortnight at least. Then we'll go on to Madeira to bask in the sunshine . . . could you zip me up the back, Mariella, please! . . . Oh, thank you! . . . Yes, it's the first time I've really been abroad, unless you could count that time I went to Brussels with the Second Company, and I was so busy I never saw anything!

144

. . . The sleeves of this dress are so tight I'm afraid one of you will have to arrange my hair and my veil. I don't know how they managed to dress themselves in medieval days!'

'The wedding went off like a dream,' Mariella said, when she wrote to Caroline, who was so busy she hadn't been able to get up for it. 'The church was decorated with mimosa sent by air from Italy by Toni Rossini, the dancer and choreographer. He's a great friend of both Veronica and Jane. Jane looked like a fairy princess or perhaps, I should say, snow queen! Her white velvet dress was cut on medieval lines, with tight sleeves, and a long train embroidered with lilies and Christmas roses in rhinestones and *diamanté*. It glittered softly, just like frost on snow. She wore a diaphanous veil of misty tulle, held in place by a coronet of real stephanotis and orange blossom, and carried a bouquet of white roses and jasmine.

'I must tell you about the awful bridesmaid flap! Little Meg Mainwaring got measles at the last minute, and Gillian (who's frightfully shy) wouldn't walk up the aisle without her. So, at the eleventh hour – almost literally – Patience thought of a friend of hers, a ballet dancer called Ella. I forget her other name. Anyway, she came up from London on the night train with Mother, and stepped into the breach, so all was well. When I first saw Ella I thought she was awfully plain and pale, but on the day she really looked lovely. I expect it's partly the way she moves. Ballet training *does* tell, doesn't it? I've lived to be grateful to Mummy for making me learn, even though I loathed it at the time, and should have hated to take it up professionally.

'I'm writing this letter in the smoking-room, after seeing Jane and Guy off at the airport, so you can't say I've kept you waiting! Actually the smoking-room is the only corner of the house where you can sit down and be reasonably certain of not sitting on a piece of wedding cake or a crumb of icing! The caterers are rushing about everywhere clearing up the mess. The house is so full of flowers it's like a flower show! Veronica and Sebastian sent up masses of chrysanthemums from the Bracken hothouses, and of course we've got lots here of our own. Then, dear Toni sent freesias and a lot of other things from Italy, as well as the mimosa for the church, and someone living in the Isles of Scilly sent Aunt Carol twelve boxes of daffodils! Provided you don't look out of the windows at the snow on the hills, you'd think it was spring!

'Now I must stop writing and get ready for tonight's festivities. There's to be a dance in the village hall for everyone. Not *our* village hall, though, because it isn't big enough, so it's to be at Hordon where Guy lives. There is to be another wedding cake, and we shall all drink the health of the bride and bridegroom. Patience Eliot and little Ella whatshername (the bridesmaid I told you about) are going to dance – professionally, I mean – and I've got a lovely new frock. It's a pale-green chiffon with a very wide skirt, and a lovely draped bodice embroidered with *diamanté*. I must look my very prettiest, because Robin Campbell, Guy's best man, will be there, and, of course, Nigel. I often wear green. Nigel once said it was my colour! But what was a long time ago. He doesn't often bother to say nice things to me now. We know each other too well, he says. I suppose it's true.

'Well, now I really *must* stop. With much love to Angelo and yourself,

'Mariella.'

Chapter 7

The Ball

It was a good idea, thought Mariella, to finish up a wedding with a ball. One didn't feel nearly so flat! She was in her bedroom dressing, and she was all by herself, since the young bridesmaid, Gillian, had been taken home by her mother who thought Gillian was too young, at eleven, for a grown-up dance. Patience and Ella had gone back to Dewburn to pack, because Patience had to return to London on the midnight train to be ready for a rehearsal the following day, and Ella was travelling with her. Their suitcases were to be put into the car, so that they could go straight from the dance-hall to the station.

'Now shall I wear my jade necklace to match my dress?' said Mariella aloud, 'or the glittering pendant, Guy's bridesmaids' gift?' She tried the effect of both in mirror, and chose the necklace. After all, she'd worn the pendant already that day with her bridesmaid's dress. 'Besides,' she added, 'everyone admires my jade necklace.' The truth was that Nigel had once remarked: 'Quite attractive, that jade thing, Mariella!' and Mariella had never forgotten. She was still under the spell Nigel had cast over her.

'They say an event that begins badly always ends well,' thought Mariella. 'I certainly hope it's true tonight, because so far the evening has been an awful flop!'

Poor Mariella! Everything had gone wrong! First of all, Robin Campbell had asked her if he might call for her and take her over to Hordon in his car, and she hadn't accepted for fear Nigel asked her. Then, of course, Nigel *hadn't* asked her, so here she was in the big family car, wedged in unromantically between her mother and Aunt Carol! Her uncle was in front with Martin, the Fosters' chauffeur-gardener.

Soon after the dance began Nigel appeared and, at his side, dressed in a very sophisticated gown of black lace, held on one white shoulder by a casual bunch of red roses, stepped a dazzling blonde. Nigel had danced with the apparition solidly all the evening, except for one Bradford barn-dance. He'd asked Mariella for that, and for the two minutes that they danced together, he had joked about it.

'Oh, hullo, Mariella, old girl! Mind if I ask you for the Bradford? Daren't ask anybody else, matter of fact, but of course I knew *you* wouldn't mind.'

Mariella sighed. For months, now, she'd looked forward to this evening. Why, she'd once even thought that Nigel might ask her to marry him in the sitting-out room! She knew, now, that he wouldn't.

Robin Campbell hadn't turned up yet. Of course, Mariella couldn't blame him, since she'd refused his escort, but she did wish he would come. It wasn't that she had any lack of partners – she was, indeed, very popular – but none of them were a patch on Robin when it came to an Eight-some Reel, or any of the Scottish dances. Then at last she saw him, and her heart missed a beat, so splendid did he look in his Highland dress. He positively towered over Mariella, as he asked her for the next dance. The top of her head only just came up to the magnificent silver brooch fastening his lace cravat. So tall, so strong, so very, very kind, thought Mariella, a little comfort stealing into her sore heart. You knew exactly where you were with Robin! He wouldn't blow hot one minute and cold the next! You could depend on Robin.

Then suddenly a wicked idea came into Mariella's head

– a thought quite unlike her usual sunny thoughts, but then, you must agree, that poor Mariella had had a lot to put up with. There was every excuse for her to have wicked thoughts! She would make Nigel jealous!

For a second she thought of taking Robin into her confidence. Then, after one glance into his steady, blue eyes, she decided against it. Robin was altogether too big – oh, not only in stature, but in character – to descend to such subterfuge! All the same, she would make him her unwitting accomplice. It didn't occur to her that Robin Campbell saw more with those blue eyes of his than she imagined. He saw in Mariella a very unhappy girl, and he guessed her plan the moment she said: 'Dance the Eightsome Reel with me, Robin! And the Gay Gordons after that. Please, *please*, Robin! Dance with me lots! Dance with me all the time!'

'It is a pleasure, Mariella,' said Robin in his slow, deliberate voice, and he led her on to the floor.

Meanwhile Ella was having her own troubles. She'd met Timothy Roebottom again at the wedding ceremony, and he hadn't recognized her. To be sure, he had wondered for a moment where he'd met the girl before – something in her pale, plain little face rang a bell – but he couldn't place her. Finally he decided that it must have been somebody else. As for Ella – she didn't want Timothy to know who she was. She'd rather be just 'Ella', an unknown dancer from Sadler's Wells than Ella Sordy of Pit Street. To be fair to Ella, it wasn't class-consciousness on her part. She didn't want to be linked to Lily and D'reen and Me Mam, or any of her old acquaintances, to be sure, but this wasn't because they were poor. It was because she felt she hadn't – in fact, had never had – anything in common with them. Neither did she wish to be linked to Lady Bailey and the big London house. She wanted to be herself – Ella at the Wells. When Timothy asked her second name, she shook her head, and answered 'Just Ella.' Sordy might mean nothing to him – it was a common enough name, and he'd probably never heard her called by it, anyway. Still, it was best to be careful.

'I'll find out, you bet!' laughed Timothy, as they walked in perfect accord. 'I'm not going to lose sight of you after tonight!'

When he saw her dance in the interval, he renewed his half-joking vow. He certanly wouldn't lose sight of her. She was very beautiful. Strange to think that he had ever thought her plain! The dance she did – it was the waltz from *Les Sylphides* – betrayed her perfect grace. He noted – as did Irma Foster – her exquisite feet, narrow, highly arched, strong as tempered steel. He noted her softly moulded arms, her expressive face. There was no mistaking the fact that her dancing was anything but ordinary!

Irma Foster's eyes met those of Veronica Weston, and their glance said: 'You've backed a winner, my dear! Congratulations! Your little Ella is certainly a "find"!'

Les Sylphides was followed by a Hungarian peasant dance by Patience Eliot. After this Timothy went out into the frosty moonlight while Ella changed out of her ballet dress. He looked at his watch. It was close on twelve o'clock. The witching hour! The hour when Cinderella's ball dress vanished and left her in her bare feet and rags! The hour when owls hoot and bats fly, and witches ride on broomsticks! The hour . . .

And then he saw her! She was dressed in her outdoor clothes – long brown coat and little fur cap and gloves, her ballet slippers tucked under her arm, their satin ribbons dangling. She was going home! He noted the car standing at the door, its engine running, and saw that Patience was already in it, and the luggage piled on the front seat.

For a moment he stood rooted to the spot. then: 'Ella!' he shouted. 'You're not going home yet?'

'Yes – to London,' said Ella, her voice sounding high and sweet in the frosty air. 'Good-bye, Timothy. It's been so lovely.'

She jumped into the car and it shot away. Martin, the Fosters' chauffeur, wasn't waiting for any tender good-byes on the part of the young. He wasn't of a romantic turn of mind, and there was only just time to catch the train!

Timothy looked after the car in disgust. Still two hours of the dance left, and no Ella! His eyes fell on something white that gleamed softly in the moonlight. He moved forward and picked it up. It was one of her ballet shoes. She must have dropped it when she got into the car. He stood for a moment holding the incredibly small and narrow satin shoe in his hand. It just fitted nicely into his palm! Then he dropped it into his pocket. Oh, well – he'd find out who she was, and he'd write to her and tell her how beautiful he had thought her dancing, and that he had found her slipper. It would surely be quite easy to find out her name.

He found that it wasn't so easy. Everyone knew her as 'Ella'. Nobody bothered about surnames these days . . . people always known by their Christian names . . . if Timothy wanted to know the girl's name, why not look in the paper (this Richard) . . . 'all the bridesmaids' names in the paper, old chap'.

But even this plan didn't work. He bought a copy of the *Northumbrian News* next day, only to find that Jane's mother had sent the notice to the news editor days before the event, as is the usual custom with weddings, and of course the bridesmaids were listed as Mariella, Patience, Gillian, and Meg! Timothy felt nonplussed. He could, of course, write to Patience and enclose a letter for Ella, but he was much too shy to do that. It seemed to poor Timothy at that moment that Ella had gone for good!

Chapter 8

Mariella Decides

Mariella found that making Nigel jealous wasn't nearly as difficult as she'd imagined. She really enjoyed dancing with Robin, and she couldn't help knowing that the two of them were the centre of attraction whenever they danced any of the popular Scottish dances. All the onlookers gathered round to watch their set, and Mariella overheard several flattering comments on 'Robin Campbell, that tall Highlander, and Mariella Foster, the pretty girl with the auburn hair and the lovely green dress.' Yes, she really had a very enjoyable evening, in spite of Nigel's conduct. So it was evidently true about an evening that began badly! Robin behaved almost as if he knew what was required of him, thought Mariella, giving her tall partner a grateful smile after a particularly thrilling set of 'Drops of Brandy'. Yes, he played up beautifully, his blue eyes lingering upon his partner's shining hair and wide, generous mouth. It never occurred to Mariella that perhaps Himself of Inveross wasn't finding the task she had set him (unbeknown, of course) difficult, either!

As for Nigel – his handsome face grew darker and darker. For one thing, his partner – the striking fair girl in the black frock – had gone home.

'Her husband came for her,' said Robin to Mariella, as they passed Nigel standing by himself at the top of the room.

'Her h-husband?' faltered Mariella.

'Oh, yes – did you not know? He does not dance, but

152

his wife loves it, which is a pity I always think. Nice fellow, McFarlane. I knew him at Edinburgh.'

A wave of anger surged over Mariella. Her evening had been spoilt – at least, it would have been but for Robin – and all because of a married woman! Then her sense of humour prevailed and she began to laugh. It was really very funny. Here was she trying to make Nigel jealous, and all the time . . .

'What is the matter?' asked Robin.

'Oh – just something!' laughed Mariella. 'Nothing to do with you, Robin. Matter of fact, I was thinking of Nigel—'

'Yes, he does look rather annoyed,' said Robin. 'I fancy he is coming over to ask you for a dance and, by the determined look on his face, you will not get out of it this time!' The last time Mariella had declared she had a head-ache and had sat out the dance with Robin in the little sitting-out room.

'Oh, there you are, Mariella!' Nigel exclaimed, coming up to them. 'Every time I look for you to ask you for a dance, you seem to disappear! Gay's gone home—'

'You mean Mrs McFarlane?'

Nigel looked a little taken aback.

'Yes. Do you know her? She's the most awful nuisance! Her husband won't take her to dances – doesn't dance himself – so she asked me to partner her for this one. I had no idea she didn't know a soul here and that I'd have to dance with her all the blooming time. It's tied me up prop-erly. Girl must be bats!'

'You seemed to be enjoying it,' ventured Mariella.

'Oh, I made the best of a bad job, you know,' said Nigel off-handedly. 'The best of a bad job. Had to pretend I was having a good time. Anyway, she's gone home now, so I'm gloriously free! I feel as if I'd just been let out of school, ha, ha! What about the next dance, Mariella?'

'I'm so sorry, Nigel, but Robin—' began Mariella, giving

the young man an appealing glance.

'Mariella is engaged to me for the Spanish Waltz,' said Robin promptly.

'Well, the one after, then? Now you can't say you're engaged for *that*, Mariella. It's an "extra", and I've just asked the band to put it on especially for us. It's the Gay Gordons.'

'Very well,' said Mariella. There was no point in holding out any longer. It was only too obvious that her plan had succeeded. Nigel was looking at Himself of Inveross with open dislike.

'That fellow takes a lot upon himself, doesn't he,' he remarked as they danced away.

'Hush, Nigel – he'll hear you! Robin has been most awfully kind to me all the evening. All the time you were dancing with Gay—'

'Oh, Lord, I've explained about that, haven't I?' said Nigel. 'I know it was a bit rough on you, Mariella, old girl, but surely you can understand. You can *trust* a chap. You know, don't you, that there's no one I would rather dance with than you? Why, I've been looking forward to this dance for ages.'

'Have you, Nigel?' Mariella said wistfully. How she longed to believe him, but she wasn't sure. She wasn't sure. She would keep up the deception a little longer. When, at the end of the evening, Nigel offered to drive her home, she told him she was going with her mother and Aunt Carol in the family car.

'Well, I do think you might let me drive you,' grumbled Nivel. 'I've been thinking about it for long enough. Oh, well, I suppose if you won't, you won't! I shall just have to bear the disappointment, that's all.'

And now Mariella had to explain to Robin what had happened, because she wasn't sure where her mother and Aunt Carol were. For all she knew they might have gone home already, knowing that she would be brought home safely by someone – if not by Nigel, by Himself of Inveross.

'I am not seeing your mother and aunt in the dance-hall,' said Robin, looking round. 'If you will be collecting your wrap I shall go to the car-park and see if your car has gone. If they are not there I can drive you home, myself.'

So it happened that Mariella was standing on the threshold of the village hall, ready dressed in her short, white, fur cape, when Nigel appeared. She noticed that his little sports car was parked at the bottom of the steps.

'I thought you said you were going home with Aunt Carol?' said Nigel.

'So I am. At least, I may be. Robin has just gone to find out—' began Mariella, when Nigel cut her short.

'Aunt Carol and your mother went home ages ago,' he said. 'I've been making inquiries. I see what it is, Mariella – you're going home with Campbell.'

'I expect I am, if what you say is true,' answered Mariella. 'After all, I must go home with *someone*, mustn't I?'

'Quite so!' Nigel said, his mouth tightening. 'You're going home with *me*. I'm not standing any more of this nonsense. Get in, Mariella!' He nodded towards his car.

'Oh, but Robin will—'

'Hang Robin! Are you going to do as I say?'

Mariella shook her head.

'It would be most awfully rude, Nigel, when Robin has gone to find out for me. Besides—'

It was the 'besides' that decided Nigel. What did she mean by 'besides'? He was hanged if he'd allow that great, gaunt Scot to run off with Mariella! Mariella was *his* girl. The Monkhouses' motto was: 'What I have, I hold,' and by jove, it was true! He intended to hold Mariella! He bent towards her and swept her into his arms in full view of a group of fascinated girls who were waiting for their partners to collect them. The next minute he had tossed her lightly over the low door of the car and the engine was running.

Lost in a dream of delight, Mariella snuggled down under the rug that Nigel had so determinedly tucked round her. How lovely to be put into a car, willy-nilly, by someone you adored! How romantic to be run away with, when the one thing you wanted in life was to be with the person who was abducting you!

The lights of Hordon villaged flashed past and vanished in the darkness. The hedgerows and drystone walls raced by. The shoulder of Ravens Eyrie loomed darkly to the left, and the little fir wood to the north of Monks Hollow shut out the frosty stars. The car's powerful headlamps picked out familiar landmarks – the little tarn, beloved of waterfowl, its black waters frozen over; the rough old stone bridge over the Hallow Burn, with the frost glittering like strings of tinsel on its parapet; the tall Scotch fir that had been struck by lightning, only half a mile from Mariella's home, the dyke at the top of the hill where the rabbits play on moonlit nights. . .

'*Nigel!*' shrieked Mariella in horror. 'Nigel, *stop!* Stop, this minute!'

Nigel, frightened by the urgency in her voice, jammed on his brakes, and the car stopped so suddenly that Mariella was thrown forward against the windscreen, and the breath nearly knocked out of her.

'What on earth's the matter?'

Mariella pointed.

'Oh, Nigel! . . . *Look!* It's something caught in one of those beastly traps. I think it's a cat!'

'Good Lord! Do you mean to say you stopped me like that just because you saw a blessed cat in a trap! Most likely it's only a rabbit, anyway.'

'Well, what if it is? What about the rabbit? It's got feelings, hasn't it? They ought to be forbidden by law – the horrible things! You should hear what they think about

gin-traps at college! No decent vet has a good word to say
for them. The poor rabbits lying there all night with their
legs nearly torn off! Foxes getting caught in them, and
pulling them up and crawling away to die by inches! Cats
– dogs. . .' All this time Mariella was struggling to open
the car door.

'Don't be an idiot, Mariella! You can't go letting things
out of traps at this time of night, and in a dance dress!
You'll get it all messed up!'

'Well, *you* get it out, then.'

'Me? Not jolly likely! If it's a cat – and it looks like one
– I'd get scratched to bits letting it out. Blessed savage,
cats, I can tell you! Don't like cats at the best of times. . .
Here! Stay where you are, Mariella!'

But Nigel found that there was a vast difference between
putting a girl into a car when she wanted to be put in it,
and keeping her there when she didn't want to be kept!
There was a short, sharp struggle, and Mariella had wren-
ched open the door and was away towards the nearest gate.
She looked a strange figure with her long chiffon dress held
up in one hand, and her white fur cape flying open to
disclose bare shoulders and the glitter of her jade necklace
in the frosty moonlight.

'Oh, the poor little thing! The poor little thing!' she said,
almost weeping, as she reached the hole in the bankside
where a small, half-grown black and white kitten lay on the
ground, struggling to escape from the cruel steel jaws that
had broken and mangled its little white front paw. 'Oh,
the beastly, beastly thing! Darling kitten, I'll get you out
somehow!'

But it was easier said than done, and it was Nigel,
following in his own time, who finally forced open the trap
by standing on it with one firm foot, while Mariella tenderly
lifted out the captive.

'Well, now I hope you're satisfied?' he said crossly. 'I

wouldn't have done that for anybody else, Mariella, I can tell you! It's just a wonder the little beast didn't claw me to death. Now you'd better turn your back and let me wring its neck. It certainly won't catch mice any more – its leg's broken in several places – and that's the only use for cats. Hand it over!'

Mariella looked down at the kitten in her arms. It was licking her hand and purring feebly.

'Thank goodness,' she said, half to herself, 'that I'm going to be a vet! Although I've only just started, I know enough to help to patch up this poor little animal's leg, even if it will have to go about mostly on three legs for the rest of its days. I'm taking it straight over to Robin. He'll be home by this time, and we can see to it together.'

Nigel stiffened.

'Robin Campbell! So that's it, is it?'

'I don't know what you mean – "so that's it, is it". Robin is a veterinary surgeon – he's the person I'm most in need of at the moment. I'm going over to his surgery straight away.'

'Not in my car you aren't,' declared Nigel. 'Anyway, you can't start performing operations in a ball dress.'

'What do I care about my stupid dress when there's work to be done?' flashed Mariella. 'But I'll take it off, of course. Robin will lend me an overall—'

'Look here,' broke in Nigel, 'you can't go dashing off to strange men's homes in the middle of the night and taking off your clothes. I forbid it!'

'Don't be so stuffy and old-fashioned!' burst out Mariella. 'You talk like the hero of a Victorian novel! I'm not going to Robin's *home* – it's in Scotland – I'm going to his surgery. Anyway, I don't have to ask you what I can or can't do.'

'Oh, yes, you do,' countered Nigel. 'Because you're my girl. I'm going to marry you, Mariella! So now what do you say?'

They stood facing each other over the kitten's body. It was really very melodramatic, thought Mariella afterwards – Nigel, so tall and masterful, and she with her long chiffon dress trailing on the frosty grass. He'd asked her to marry him at last! Not in the warmth of a ballroom, or at a race-meeting, or at any of the places you might have expected, but out here in this frosty field at two o'clock in the morning, with the kitten between them licking its poor. bloody paw and purring! A little black and white kitten to be the unconscious means of Nigel's proposing to her at last! It was enough to make, yes, a cat laugh! So thought Mariella afterwards.

But the kitten had done something else, too. Suddenly Mariella felt that something that had bound her to Nigel for a very long time – a kind of invisible chain – had snapped. It was as if a spell which had lain over her nearly all her life had been lifted, and she saw Nigel for what he really was. She still loved him with one side of her, but the other side – the important side – knew that she couldn't marry him – not even now that he'd asked her. She knew that he wasn't worthy to be loved at all, that he was cruel, and selfish, and conceited.

'I'm going, Nigel,' she said, with a little sigh – a sigh for the Nigel she had thought he was. 'I'm going now, and I'm sorry but I can't marry you. Good-bye, Nigel.'

'Well, if you take it like that – right-ho, Mariella, good-bye!' said Nigel. 'I shall come over to Monks Hollow tomorrow for my answer, and I shall hope to find you in a more sensible frame of mind by then.'

He turned back toward his car and vowed that he'd win Mariella back. Robin Campbell, indeed! Yes, he'd marry Mariella, and teach her who was master! She was a very pretty girl and he'd always admired her. Besides, she adored him – always had! Couldn't have another fellow running off with one's girl! Robin Campbell, indeed! He'd settle all that tomorrow. He'd get her back!

But the waning moon, sailing in the clear, night sky, had a one-sided smile, and a little cold breeze ruffling the tops of the fir trees sighed softly and murmured that he wouldn't!

Chapter 9

After the Ball

Ella's year at the Wells passed by quickly now. Already it was nearing the end of the summer term and her fellow-students – Patience, Susan, and Jessica – were preparing to go home. At least Susan was going to stay with an aunt who lived in Hampshire for a fortnight before she began rehearsals for the coming season, and Jessica was flying back to Johannesburg to teach in a school. Patience was spending her holiday in Paris with a school friend, and was then coming back to London to begin rehearsals down at the Wells. She had got a part in *Façade*.

Ella, herself, hadn't got a part in anything. A list had gone up on the notice board in the Winter Garden, and all her classmates were down as mice and rats, or peasant girls in the new production of the *Sleeping Beauty*, or one of the other ballets.

'I suppose I'm not good enough,' thought Ella wistfully. It was true she wasn't really as advanced as most of them. After all, she had only been learning ballet for eighteen months. Still, she couldn't help being a little disappointed – and also apprehensive. She wondered if her scholarship would be renewed. Nobody had said anything about it, nor had they praised her dancing. Even Mr Delahaye more often shouted at her than approved her, and Ella wasn't knowledgeable enough to realize that shouts and criticism from a ballet master were worth any amount of praise! And as for the other classes, nobody seemed to notice her in them at all. She remained in the back row, diligently practising the steps and *enchainements*, trying to follow those students she thought were the best, striving all the time for perfection. Perfection was the only thing good enough for Ella. Even if she never reached it, she would always strive for it.

There was a great deal of rivalry amongst the students. They eyed each other jealously, and every newcomer was looked upon with suspicion. Who knew – she might prove to be another Margot Fonteyn! They never resented Ella. For one thing, she wasn't advanced enough to cause jealousy. For another, she never tried to rival anybody herself. She just worked away on her own, watching the best performance, it is true, but never with any sense of rivalry – not as far as her fellow-students were concerned. Movements were her rivals rather than people!

The day before term ended, Ella took her courage in her hands, and waited for Miss Peters, her form mistress, after the history class.

'Miss Peters,' she said. 'May I speak to you?'

Miss Peters was busy with the end-of-term reports. She nodded her head absent-mindedly.

'Yes, Ella?'

'Am I to stay here next year?' asked Ella, with the courage of desperation.

Miss Peters hardly paused in her task of addressing envelopes. She was going to have a job to get them done in time.

'No, dear,' she answered. 'Your parents have been informed.'

Ella gulped. Then *this* was why she remained unnoticed in the back row! *This* was why Gilbert shouted at her and criticized her! *This* was why she hadn't got any parts in the ballets! Her scholarship wasn't going to be renewed. She hadn't made the progress expected of her.

'Run away, dear,' said Miss Peters, a frown creasing her forehead. It wasn't anything to do with Ella, but she had very nearly put Susan Barker's report in Mrs Stevens' envelope! This end-of-term rush! She'd be glad when it was over and she was having a well-earned vacation on the Continent. Meanwhile, this child – this promising child whom she'd been told was 'one to watch' – was still standing there, obviously waiting for something.

'Take these books along to the staff room, dear,' said Miss Peters, 'and leave them on the bench. Oh, and shut the door, Ella, please.'

'Yes, Miss Peters,' whispered Ella.

For a moment the mistress was conscience-stricken. The poor child looked unhappy. She was probably homesick! She almost rushed after her to find out the reason; then restrained herself. If one ran after all the children who were homesick, or unhappy, in a ballet school, one would never stop running! A ballet school is full of heartache. How could it be otherwise?

If you had told Miss Peters that the misery in Ella's face was because she 'wasn't good enough', she would have laughed. Good enough? Why, she was quite the best in the Junior School – excepting none! She worked *too* hard. There was a danger of her becoming strained, and she was far too precious to Sadler's Wells for that to be allowed to happen. She must have a good holiday, with no work at all, and no parts in any ballets – for the present, that is. It never occurred to Miss Peters that Ella, herself, didn't know this. That Ella, so modest and retiring, might not realize just how good she was. She never thought to tell her. And so the misunderstanding began!

That night in bed, when all the other students had gone, Ella cried bitterly. Outside in the square, London's night life went on as usual. Taxis droned past, doors opened and shut, voices laughed softly, cars rolled by with a soft whine, several clocks in the neighbourhood chimed on different notes, the measured tread of a policeman on his beat sounded on the pavement below. Ella had been homesick many times, but always she had had the thought that here, in London, she had her dancing. Now she had nothing.

'I want to go home!' she sobbed into her pillow. They say that 'distance lends enchantment to the view'! It was certainly true in Ella's case. She forgot all about the dirt and squalor of Pit Street, and only remembered the happy things that had happened to her when she lived there. The times she had gone out 'brambling' with her schoolmates on the purple moors, high above the pit chimneys. The times she had played hopscotch with Lily and D'reen on the pavement on those first warm spring evenings when the nights were beginning to 'draw out'. She remembered the Sunday School; the ballet class in the church hall, Timothy Roebottom and her very first ballet dress.

The next day she crept about the house, such a forlorn little figure that even the lordly Grayson unbent and asked her if she would like to watch the television in the kitchen.

'I don't suppose her ladyship would mind,' he added to Jenny. 'And anyway, she's in Scotland for the weekend, and what she doesn't know won't hurt her!'

That night, after she had had her lonely supper in the big, empty dining-room, Ella made up her mind. She would go home! After all, if she had to go sometime, it might as well be now. She had heard some of the girls talking about the cheapness of travel by bus. She thought that she had just enough money. She would slip out when the house was quiet and they thought her in bed and asleep, and find out if it was enough to take her home by bus. She would leave a letter for kind Lady Bailey, thanking her for all she had done, and saying how sorry she was not to have been a success, and that she had gone home, and please not to worry about her.

Thus it happened that, on the following morning, a small

figure got wearily down from the long-distance bus in the Haymarket, Newcastle, and asked the conductor where the Blackheath bus went from.

'It goes from o'er yonder, hinny,' said the man, pointing. 'But ye've got a half an oo'r's wait. Ye'd best gan to the snack bar, and warm yersel' up wi' a cup o'tea.'

'Yes, I will,' said Ella. 'And thank you very much. It's lovely to hear you talk!'

The man looked after her. Lovely to hear him talk? 'Noo what did the bairn mean by that?' he said aloud. He had no time to find out, however, as his bus moved off at that moment and he had to jump on it or be left behind.

Ella reached Blackheath at ten o'clock. It was a Saturday morning and the streets were full of children playing on the pavements, children running errands for their mothers, children running over the roads in front of motor cars, playing that forbidden but enchanting game of 'last across'. There were no gardens or playgrounds down here, such as there were up in the New Estate.

Above the sprawling village the pit chimneys reared their black heads, belching forth smoke, the slag-heaps smouldered, the machinery clanked and groaned and ground its teeth like a monster of steel. Oh, how dirty and depressing it was! In the darkness it might have a certain satanic majesty but, in the cold light of day, it was squalid beyond belief. So thought Ella – now that she was here!

Pit Street looked meaner than ever. She saw now the unpainted window-sills and doors; the uneven road of cobblestones, the forest of television aerials ornamenting the rooftops. They were like a flock of crazy storks, thought Ella!

At last she reached number 113. At the door stood a girl – a large, coarse girl with bold, black eyes, red cheeks, and fat red hands. It couldn't – it *couldn't* be Lily! But it was! And behind her stood another girl, grown up beyond belief. D'reen! Ella had grown up, too, but not like this. Her small, pale face had a tinge of pink in it now, her cheeks had rounded, but it was still the face of a child – young and innocent. Lily and D'reen were buxom young women, although they were both only just in their teens.

'Hullo!' faltered Ella. 'I thought – I thought I should like to – to come home for a bit, and – see you all.'

Lily and D'reen gave a squeal and vanished indoors. She heard them calling shrilly:

'Mam! Mam! Here's our Ella! She's come back from Lunnon, and she talks that funny!'

Ella went into the front-room. Yes, it was just the same – very clean, a little more shabby, very patriotic (the Royal Family still reigned supreme on the walls!). But oh, how it had shrunk! After Lady Bailey's big London house the front-room at Pit Street was like a small, square box! She wasn't left long by herself, however. In another moment Me Mam appeared, her hands steaming, as usual, from the inevitable washing-up.

'Well, I never!' said Me Mam. 'Talkin' about seeing ghosts!'

'I've come back, Mother,' said Ella. 'I wasn't good enough, so I've come home.'

'You oughta ha'let us know you was comin',' said Me Mam in genuine distress. 'There ain't nowhere for you to sleep. When you went off to Lunnon we 'ad to dee summat to make ends meet, so we divided our Lily and our D'reen's room, and took in a lodger. It taks a shoehorn to get our Lily and our D'reen in that room now, and it's nobbut a single bed.'

'Oh,' said Ella. 'I never thought.'

'You oughta ha' let us know you'd got the sack,' repeated Me Mam. She stood looking at Ella, not offering to kiss her. This wasn't because she didn't want to – after all, although she looked different, and talked 'la-de-la' she was still 'our Ella' – it was because she didn't dare. There was something dignified about Ella at that moment.

'Anyways,' went on Mrs Sordy, 'ye'll ha' to gan up to the Cottage 'Omes and ax if it'll be all right for ye to come back 'ere. I don't want no trouble. They'll mebbie jib aboot three on ye in that small room. They're that hygienic! Mebbie it'd be best if they kep ye up there the neet, but if they wunna, then ye can come back 'ere and sleep on the fl-oar. A'll borrow some rugs and that from somewhere. A'll not see ye beat.'

'Thank you, Mother,' said Ella. 'Good-bye, then.'

'Ta-ta,' said Me Mam. She plucked up courage, pulled the girl towards her, and kissed her. After all, she was nobbut a bairn, and she looked real miserable! 'A'll not see ye beat,' she repeated. Behind her stood Lily and D'reen, nudging each other and giggling.

Slowly Ella walked back down Pit Street, and the children stopped playing, and stood watching her in silent curiosity.

The Cottage Homes were up beyond the church. The big, brick building dominated the hill, on the slopes of which the New Estate was built. Ella had only been there once, and that was for an interview just before she went to London, but she remembered that there was a short cut up a steep and muddy lane by the side of the church. She found the lane, and was just about to turn into it, when she came face to face with a young man walking in the oposite direction. Their eyes met – his blue and friendly; hers dark with trouble. Then he exclaimed:

'Ella! Whatever are you doing here?'

'I live here,' said Ella. 'At least, I used to live here.'

'Wait! Don't tell me – it's coming back!' exclaimed Timothy Roebottom. 'Why, you're the little girl in the church – the one who wanted a ballet dress. When I met you again at Guy Charlton's wedding, I knew I'd seen you somewhere before, but I just couldn't fix you.'

'I didn't want you to,' Ella said simply.

'Oh, but why not?'

'I didn't want you to think of me – like I was then,' faltered Ella. 'I'd rather be just Ella – if you don't mind.'

'Not at all,' Timothy said politely. 'It's all the same to me. But I do think I ought to know your surname now – just for convenience, you know – even if I never call you by it.'

'Well, you might think it was Sordy,' said Ella. 'I did myself for a long time – until I found out that my mother wasn't my real mother.'

'Clear as mud!' pronounced Timothy.

'You see, I found out not so long ago that I'm an orphan,' went on Ella. 'My mother died when I was born, and my father was – or is – Italian. They told me at the Cottage Homes that my real name is Rosetti.'

'Well, that's a whole lot better than Sordy,' declared Timothy candidly. 'D'you mind if I walk a little way with you, Miss er – Rosetti? I've got something with me that belongs to you.'

'To me?' echoed Ella in surprise. Whatever could Timothy Roebottom have that belonged to her?

'Yes, here it is.' He drew out of his pocket a small white satin ballet shoe.

'Oh, so *that's* what became of it!' said Ella. 'I often wondered where it had gone to. I must have dropped it.'

'Yes – at Jane's dance, and I picked it up. Just like Cinderella! It's been in my pocket ever since.' They had come to a stile leading into a field over which the path wound up to the Cottage Homes. 'May I try it on you? Must keep up the Cinderella tradition, you know!' He put his two hands round her waist and lifted her onto the stile. So slender was she that his hands nearly met. Then he stood waiting while she took off one of her shoes. 'Now you must let me put it on. I ought to go down on my knees,

168

by rights, but it's rather muddy, so you'll have to let me off!' He bent down and fitted the ballet shoe on her stock-inged foot. 'Yes, it's yours all right, Cinderella! And now I suppose I shall have to give it back to you?'

'Please,' said Ella. 'You see, the other one's no use without it.'

'No, I suppose it isn't. Pity, though! I'd got sort of used to it nestling in my pocket. I'd begun to think it belonged to a fairy! I said to myself: "Timothy Roebottom – no human being could ever get *that* on – not even Cinderella! You've been dancing with a fairy – one that vanishes at the midnight hour!" Well, "Ella at the Wells," – if that's how you like to be addressed – what brings you to your native haunts? Is it a case of the criminal revisiting the scene of his crime?'

The misery came back into the girl's face. For the last few moments her joy at seeing Timothy again had almost made her forget the tragedy that had befallen her.

'Oh, Timothy – don't joke,' she said. 'I'm in the most awful trouble.' Then out it all came. The scholarship that lasted a year; Miss Peters' pronouncement that she wasn't to go back, the list of ballets, and her name not on it; her flight from London and now . . .

'And now there's no room for you in Pit Street?' said Timothy. 'Well, don't let that worry you, Ella. You just come along to the Vicarage. My mother will be as pleased as anything to put you up, take it from me! I'll let you into a secret,' he added. 'My mother is keen on ballet, so keen that she used to draw *you*, when you had classes in the church hall ages ago. She sent her drawings up to Courtneys the publishers, and they've given her several commissions. So, I assure you, you'll be *most* popular with my mother! The money she gets for her drawings has made all the difference up at the Vicarage!'

Chapter 10

The End of the Story

At about ten-thirty that night, just when the 'V'riety Show' on television was finishing, Pit Street was electrified by the sight of a long, low, black car which drew up at number 113. 'The police,' thought Mrs Sordy's neighbours, looking out from behind their curtains. But the young man who got out of the car was obviously no policeman, though it was equally obvious that he was no ordinary person. He was in full evening dress and, over the top was slung an opera cloak which, when the wind caught it, showed a white satin lining. Sebastian Scott had not grown less spectacular as he had grown older and more famous! He knocked peremptorily on the door of number 113 with a silver-mounted cane, and stood waiting.

To say that Me Mam was taken aback is putting it mildly! Like her neighbours, she thought at first that her visitor was a policeman. Now she was pretty sure he was either an escaped lunatic, or 'one of them spaceship men' Our Lily and Our D'reen read about in their comics. He stood on the steps and looked her up and down with a pair of glittering dark blue eyes. 'It fair turned me stummick over!' she told Mrs Rickerby afterwards.

'I have come for Ella,' he said at length.

'She ain't 'ere,' said Mrs Sordy. 'She were 'ere, but she ain't now.'

'Well, where is she, my good woman?' demanded Sebastian. 'Where is she? Be quick and tell me!'

'There wasn't no room for 'er 'ere,' explained Mrs Sordy,

'so she's gone up to the Cottage Homes—'

'Do you realize,' said Sebastian, wagging a finger in front of Ella's Mam's nose, 'that if this gifted child is lost, the world will weep, and it will be *your* doing?'

'I never made no one weep,' declared Mrs Sordy indignantly. 'That's a downright lie, sir!'

'Figuratively speaking,' said Sebastian softly. 'Figuratively speaking. Do you know, Mrs Sordy, that this child is one of the most promising dancers Sadler's Wells has ever had? Do you know that she is going to be a classical ballerina second to none? And you – *you* have lost her!'

'No, I never!' said Mrs Sordy. 'I telt her that if the Cottage 'Omes winna tak' 'er in, she's to come back 'ere, and sleep on the floor along o' Lily and D'reen.'

'The exquisite Ella Rosetti to sleep on the floor – along o' Lily and D'reen!' murmured Sebastian, half to himself. 'The pearl among the swine!'

'My bairns ain't no swine!' exclaimed Mrs Sordy in righteous wrath. 'Don't you dare call my bairns names, young man – whoever you are! My bairns are as good as anybody else's bairns. Don't you dare!'

'My dear good woman – there is nothing I would not dare in the preservation of the arts. Nothing!' declared Sebastian. 'If, through you, this peerless dancer is lost to the world, woe betide you, Mrs Sordy. Woe betide you! That is all I have to say.' He turned on his heel and stalked back to the car, his cloak swinging. The inhabitants of Pit Street drew in their breaths with a communal 'Oo!' Never had they seen anyone the least like Sebastian Scott! In this they were not peculiar. The young conductor was said to be unique. There was only one Sebastian Scott!

'Yes, my dear,' said Sebastian, a short while later when, by means of exhaustive inquiries of the local youth standing at street corners, he arrived at Blackheath Vicarage, 'you have caused a vast amount of trouble. Because of you, the

171

telephone wires have been humming! Lady Bailey has been spending pounds on trunk calls from Scotland! My wife has been frantic with anxiety! The Wells has been shattered! As for me' – he gesticulated dramatically at his clothes – 'I have come here straight from the City Hall in Newcastle, where I was conducting my symphony.'

'I'm very sorry, Mr Scott,' said Ella, 'but I don't see why anyone should worry – least of all the Wells.'

'Not worry when one of their most promising dancers runs away?'

'You don't mean it, Mr Scott,' said Ella. 'They told me I wasn't to go back. Miss Peters said so herself.'

'My stupid child – my dear little blockhead,' said Sebastian affectionately, 'she meant, no doubt, that you were not to go back to the Junior School. I have here in my pocket the report the Wells has sent to my wife. Shall I read it? Then, perhaps, you will be convinced. . . "This pupil is one of the most promising we have had for a very long time. In our opinion no money spent over her dancing education will be wasted. We think that she will go far. She must not be forced, however. We do not wish her to appear on the stage for some time yet. We think that she should begin to work in the Senior School next term for most of the classes, so that she will have more advanced students to follow, but she must on nó account try to progress too fast. . ." Well, Ella, *now* are you satisfied? You should burst into tears, you know – tears of happiness! Veronica always does!'

But Ella had already done so!

Lorna Hill
A Dream of Sadler's Wells £2.25

This is the first of the Wells series in which we meet Veronica, who is determined to become a dancer. She is torn away from London and her ballet classes and sent to live with unsympathetic relations in Northumberland, but she manages to overcome all sorts of setbacks and finally reaches her audition for the Royal Ballet School at Sadler's Wells.

Veronica at the Wells £2.25

Veronica is now at the Sadler's Wells ballet school and her first days are exciting, even a little frightening for not everyone welcomes the talented newcomer. When she is fifteen, Veronica has the most wonderful Christmas present -- her first part at Covent Garden.

No Castanets at the Wells £2.25

After meeting the exciting young Spanish dancer Angelo Ibanez, Caroline Scott is even more determined than ever to take her dancing seriously. Eventually she follows her talented cousin, Veronica Weston, to the Sadler's Wells Ballet School. Once there, however, she becomes the despair of her teachers — all except the fierce and fiery Serge Lopokoff, for it is only in his Character classes that Caroline really comes alive. Fortunately, Angelo has never forgotten the promise he made that Christmas in Northumberland . . .

Masquerade at the Wells £2.25

Jane and Mariella Foster were cousins, with everything and nothing in common – Mariella, daughter of a prima ballerina, loved horses and dogs and the outdoor life that Jane was forced to lead. Jane was prepared to do anything for the ballet lessons which her cousin hated. A daring deception is born when Jane takes Mariella's place at an audition for Sadler's Wells Ballet School. She passes and begins a new life – as Mariella Foster! Jane loves the Wells, but fears that – one day – someone will discover her secret . . .

Jane Leaves the Wells £2.25

When Veronica Weston marries, Jane Foster steps into several of her roles – gaining instant success and admiration. Her future as a ballerina seems assured, but Jane distrusts her own good fortune, knowing that, unlike Veronica, she is not one of the 'great ones'. During an eventful midwinter visit to Scotland Jane is faced with an almost impossible choice – her dancing or her love for a rugged Northumbrian, Guy Charlton

Return to the Wells £2.25

Ella Sordy from Pit Street has become Ella Rosetti of the Sadler's Wells. Her life had taken an unexpected turn and Ella's future as a brilliant ballerina seems assured. Suddenly she is struck down by illness – an illness so grave that only the presence of her own 'prince charming' can call her back from her delirium. Timothy Roebottom speeds through the night to the bedside of the girl he loves but cannot have . . .

To follow

Rosanna Joins the Wells

When Rosanna Corelli's parents are tragically killed and her guardian Papa Angeline dies, she is reluctantly sent for by her English aunt and uncle. For Rosanna, England means only one thing – the Sadler's Wells Ballet School. But, treated like a servant by her aunt and scorned by her cousins, Rosanna is forbidden to even *think* about dancing. Undaunted, she runs away and sets out alone to make her dream come true . . .

All Pan books are available at your local bookshop or newsagent, or can be ordered direct from the publisher. Indicate the number of copies required and fill in the form below.

Send to: **CS Department, Pan Books Ltd., P.O. Box 40, Basingstoke, Hants. RG21 2YT.**

or phone: 0256 469551 (Ansaphone), quoting title, author and Credit Card number.

Please enclose a remittance* to the value of the cover price plus: 60p for the first book plus 30p per copy for each additional book ordered to a maximum charge of £2.40 to cover postage and packing.

*Payment may be made in sterling by UK personal cheque, postal order, sterling draft or international money order, made payable to Pan Books Ltd.

Alternatively by Barclaycard/Access:

Card No.

Signature:

Applicable only in the UK and Republic of Ireland.

While every effort is made to keep prices low, it is sometimes necessary to increase prices at short notice. Pan Books reserve the right to show on covers and charge new retail prices which may differ from those advertised in the text or elsewhere.

NAME AND ADDRESS IN BLOCK LETTERS PLEASE:

Name

Address

3/87